I0846712

VALERIE MASSEY GOREE

Meet Me Where the Windrush Flows

Valerie Massey Goree

This book contains subject matter that might be difficult for some readers.

Disclaimer: Bourton-on-the-Water is a real village in the Cotswolds. Cloisters and Puffitts are real cottages in the village. The author has the owners' permission to use their beautiful homes in the book. The Salmonsbury Camp Hillfort is a real place, and previous excavations did take place. However, the excavations described in the book are purely the author's creation. Some liberties have been taken with the area.

ISBN-13: 978-1-962168-41-0

What Readers Are Saying

Shadows of Time:
Read. This. Book. Even if contemporary or romantic suspense fiction isn't normally your "thing" you'll love this book. The plot line is a fascinating what if scenario that seems chillingly possible. I love that the author tied the story to the past, and real historical events are referenced, adding more credibility to the plot. The story opens with a bang and kept me turning pages to the very end. There are twists and turns that add depth and intrigue. The author obviously did her research, and I can't imagine how much study it took to become knowledgeable enough to write the book. The topic of genetics is deeply scientific, but the author wove the information into the book mostly through snippets of dialog, so I was able to understand without having to look up stuff or feel like I was reading a textbook. The book is set in the Seattle area, and the description helped me visualize the surroundings, giving me a virtual visit. The characters are well-written, and I especially love Cullen, flawed, yet likable, with an unusual set of traits. Highly recommended.

*Best-selling author, Linda Shenton Matchett.

"*Forever Under Blue Skies* made me want to visit Australia. The two mysteries woven into the story kept me turning the pages and the proposal was so romantic, I had to read it twice."

*Amazon Reader Review

Other Books By Valerie Massey Goree
Texas Suspense:
Deceive Me Once
Colors of Deceit

Stolen Lives Trilogy:
Weep in the Night
Day of Reckoning
Justice at Dawn

Stand Alone:
Forever Under Blue Skies

My Mother's Secret:
Shadows of Time
Every Hidden Thing

CHAPTER 1

Bourton-on-the-Water, Gloucestershire, England
Autumn

With the small bag of groceries casually slung over his shoulder, Logan Quinn strode across one of the stone footbridges spanning the River Windrush. The gentle waterway meandered through Bourton in no hurry to join the Dikler River south of the village. Since it was a beautiful, cool day and the fall colors were magnificent, he took his time returning to the cottage. However, the peaceful setting had been marred by three teenagers who rode bicycles up and down High Street and seemed intent on crossing all five bridges, none of which had handrails. He kept a wary eye on them as they rode along the paved area beside the river. They swerved, crossed the vehicular bridge, and zig-zagged around pedestrians on the sidewalk.

As Logan passed the outdoor seating area of The Corner Inn, a young man seated at one of the tables yelled, "Grace, your order's ready." The man looked toward the footbridge on the right of the main crossing, then turned to his companions. "Did she find her other hearing aid?"

Logan slowed his steps and noticed the woman standing on the bridge. She examined her cell phone, head down, and didn't respond to her friend. Raucous conversation alerted Logan to the teens approaching that bridge. If the young woman had lost a hearing aid, she probably wouldn't hear the oncoming assault. His frantic gaze flew from the approaching bikers to Grace. They weren't paying any attention to their surroundings and probably wouldn't consider the fate of anyone in their way.

He dropped the grocery bag, hurried toward Grace, waved, and shouted a warning, but she didn't react. He reached her, and her head jerked up as she shoved her phone into the pocket of her jeans. No sense trying to explain what he was about to do. He picked her up and carried her off the bridge just as the trio of bikers rushed across. Two even had their legs sticking out as if to knock a pedestrian into the river.

Although the Windrush meandering through the village was only a foot deep, a fall could result in injury. At first, Grace pummeled Logan with her tiny fists, then when she noticed the danger he'd spared her, she stopped and mumbled, "Thank you."

Logan made sure to face her when he replied, "You're welcome. Your friends over there say your order is ready." He couldn't help but notice sparkling dark eyes and her refined features in a pale, oval face, black hair in a ponytail, and wide bangs covering her forehead. She was five feet tall at the most, and on closer inspection, he realized she was not as young as he'd initially thought.

Grace walked over to the table where her four friends sat. They had witnessed Logan's actions. One of the party, a black man with a distinct haircut—shaved back and sides, but long curls on top—stood and held out his hand. "Brilliant save back there." They shook hands while Grace settled into the empty chair and zipped up her puffy pink jacket.

Color had returned to her cheeks. "Thank you again. Would you like to join us?" An unmistakable American accent.

Although interested in his fellow countryman…woman, he had to decline. "Thanks, but no." He pointed to his discarded bag. "I need to get the groceries back to the cottage." Just then, his phone beeped. "Sorry. This might be important." He stepped away then removed the phone from his jacket pocket and checked the text. Nothing serious. Just Mother asking when he'd be home. About to leave, he couldn't help but overhear the conversation at the table behind him.

"Do you think the bones I found might be Roman?"

Intrigue stopped him in his tracks. Roman as in Roman ruins? He had to ask. "Excuse me. I heard your question. What…where are these bones? I'm interested in Roman ruins of any kind. While we've been in England, I've visited many sites. Maybe I can help?"

"Are you an archeologist?" Grace asked.

"No, a doctor, a pediatric surgeon, but I'm taking a break to help my mother."

"Why?"

If anyone but Grace had asked, he would have

responded only with a shrug. "Staying in Bourton-on-the-Water is on her bucket list."

"What a nice son."

Debatable. Grace's reply ruffled his usual calm. His trip to the UK and away from Texas was as much for his benefit as Mother's. To hide his discomfort, he focused on the petite member of the diverse group. Not young enough to be an archeology student but he couldn't decide if Grace was the leader. To continue the conversation, he asked, "Did you locate the bones here in Bourton?"

She nodded. "I'm Dr. Grace Gentry, a visiting professor at the University of Oxford. These are my students. We've been excavating a site close to the Roman camp at Salmonsbury, and just this morning, we unearthed more skeletal remains, but none were in usual burial sites."

"What's the difference?"

Leaning over her plate, Grace forked a piece of chicken into her mouth and didn't act as if she heard him.

The black man responded. "The finds at this site haven't been officially authenticated yet, so I'd better not say."

Logan's phone buzzed again. "Sorry, that will be Mother wondering where I am. Can I um, get your names or something? I'm very interested in your find." *Not to say your professor.*

"Sure." The man handed him a card. "I'm Marcus Reid, Dr. Gentry's assistant. We'll be here a while. The find is on private land so we have no time constraints."

"Thank you. May I stop by?"

"As long as you don't interfere. We are not

equipped for amateurs."

Whew. Grace's words and the scowl she gave him put him in his place.

"Great. Thanks. Um, where are you working?"

After getting a nod from Grace, Marcus said, "Take Station Road to Cemetery Lane. Pass the carp fishing camp. Keep left. Go to the end of the lane and you'll see a parking area on your right. Walk east between the lakes. Our tent and pop-up canopy are at the far end."

"Thanks." With a bounce in his step, he walked up Victoria Street toward the cottage. Aware a man wearing a pale green jacket had been following him, Logan stopped at the corner and glanced over his shoulder. The man slipped down the walkway between the buildings. Hmm. If interested in Logan, the stalker probably knew where he lived. The unsettling feeling of being followed couldn't dampen his euphoria concerning recent events. His time in Bourton might not be as dull as he'd expected.

Opening the front door, he called, "Sorry it took me so long."

Mother set a platter of sandwich ingredients on the kitchen table. The stilton cheese had a distinctive aroma. "I was afraid the store didn't have my baps and you had to go someplace else."

"Nope." Logan deposited the contents of the cloth grocery bag onto the table. "Here are the buns and a bottle of mayonnaise." He had to agree with Mother. Baps made the best sandwiches he'd tasted in a long time. "Where's Reggie?"

"Upstairs."

Logan stepped into the foyer and hollered up the

stairs. "Lunch is ready, Reg."

Mother's good friend and traveling companion easily negotiated the steep staircase. Although stooped and silver-haired, she had more energy than Logan and Mother combined.

While assembling her sandwich, Reggie asked, "Want to eat in the conservatory?"

"Sure. The sunshine will be most welcome." Mother carried her plate out and settled at the large refectory table.

During the meal, Logan related his eventful excursion, including every sight and sound, and described the people in as much detail as he could remember. He wanted to be sure to share everything with Mother before she forgot who he was. Early onset Alzheimer's was the worst way to go.

She dabbed at her mouth with her napkin. "I'm glad you found a Roman interest in the village. That will keep you busy while I finish my crocheting. I love sitting out here. The garden is delightful. So peaceful." She gazed out the large windows and then sighed. "Just remember you don't have a stellar track record with women."

You don't have to remind me. Not married to the mother of his son. Two broken engagements. Logan hung his head as he gathered the plates and retreated to the kitchen.

Reggie carried her laptop to the conservatory along with Mother's crocheting bag. The blanket for a friend's grandbaby was about half complete. Logan hoped Mother's motor memory would allow her to finish it.

After cleaning the kitchen, he ran up the two

flights of stairs to his attic bedroom. The open windows, although small, allowed the cool air to circulate. He flopped onto the single bed, his feet hanging off the bottom. He folded his hands behind his head and stared at the beams in the A-shaped ceiling. As soon as he'd seen Grace on the bridge and became aware of her predicament, he had the instant desire to protect her. When he gazed at her pale face and felt her small fists on his chest, he wanted so much more. He was more than ready to describe his encounter as an attraction at first sight.

Aware of his awful track record and the possibility he'd never see Grace again once he left Bourton, Logan still grinned. His third day in the village had turned out to be positive.

He didn't regret taking Mother on her bucket list tour of Scotland and England, but he often craved the company of people closer to his age. Voila. Four students and their intriguing professor. He'd rented the cottage for two weeks—Mother's insistence—so he had time to get to know Grace.

Swinging his legs off the bed, he set his elbows on his knees and clasped his hands. Although he'd love to follow Grace back to Oxford when she and her team completed their excavation, Mother's needs came first. She had several places in London she wanted to visit, and then Dover and Brighton. They had open return tickets, and drawing on his professional skills, he'd gauge when to return home.

Return to what? He stood and paced to the doorway and back. His career and reputation were ruined when a colleague blamed him for his fatal misdiagnosis. Logan was not looking forward to the arduous task of clearing his name.

In the meantime, he would ask Reggie to take Mother to the Model Village tomorrow so he could visit the dig site and get to know little Dr. Gentry.

CHAPTER 2

"Why did you give that man so much detail about our site? You know we don't want random people showing up. Sir Barrette Caplan won't appreciate the public wandering around his land." Grace kept her eyes on Marcus's mouth to read his lips. The engine noise interfered with the effectiveness of her hearing aid.

He drove to the graveled area, parked, and shrugged. "Logan seemed so interested and he did save you."

He *had* rescued her, held her. The memory sent tingles to her heart. So why her criticism? Her turn to shrug. He was about the best-looking guy she'd seen in a long time, but he was arrogant. As if visiting Roman sites qualified him to help her. Before stepping out of the van, she noticed a small, tan-colored object in the foot well. Her missing hearing aid. It must have fallen out that morning. She placed it in her left ear, hitched the strap of her computer bag onto her shoulder, and followed the crew down the path to the tent covering their equipment and display tables.

Bones from two humans had been meticulously removed from their damp, earthen grave beside the lake. Marcus had taken a slew of photographs in situ and also with the remains laid out in anatomical order, and as per her directions, had documented each find in the site log. They had found enough bones to identify an adult male and an older female. The male's right hand appeared to have been cut off. The history of the site in the annex of Salmonsbury Camp would account for the missing bones. Used for centuries starting with occupants from the Middle Stone Age, about 8,000 BC, to Anglo-Saxons from 500 AD up to the Norman conquest in 1066, the skeletons could be from any of the latter centuries. Add to that, this part of the site had been used for gravel excavations in the 1960s. Who knew what damage the machines did to any remaining bones or artifacts? However, everyone was surprised to find any human remains in the area as the annex was mainly used for grazing animals.

When Sir Barrette had trees removed from the water's edge at the northeast end of the lake and began digging holes for supports for a new deck, he'd found a piece of pottery. He knew enough history about the area to contact the Cotswold Archeological Trust. They advised him to stop digging until they had evaluated the site. His sister, Grace's boss, headed the archeology department at the University of Oxford. He wanted her to lead the investigation. And he got his way. Hence, Grace's presence.

The crew's chattering cut into her concentration. She turned down the volume of her hearing aids until their conversation became only a mild roar. Why the cut-off hand? Romans did remove the right hands of soldiers who stole from civilians, but she had to keep in mind that just because the present owner of the property found a shard of pottery the archeology department at Oxford had dated to the Roman occupation, didn't mean the skeletons were from the same period.

Setting aside a femur, Grace checked her phone for an expected email. Not there. She'd interviewed for a teaching post at Brandeis University in Massachusetts and was supposed to be notified yesterday. Did no message mean no job? Her shoulders sagged. Not good enough, again. Probably lost out to an applicant who seemed more outgoing. Couldn't an introvert be just as good an anthropologist as a blabbermouth? She shook her head, remembering a previous job she applied for and the person they hired. That woman gushed words as if she were a geyser. Grace needed to be more forceful in her interviews. That was always the feedback given, but surely her experience should speak for her.

Grace knew she had a soft voice and looked more like a teenager than a thirty-five-year-old woman, but she could change none of that. She had to heed the advice and become more forceful in her presentations. Forge ahead despite her physical limitations. But truth be told, she preferred excavating sites where the bones spoke to her and they didn't care that she was hard of hearing, or only four-feet-eleven-inches tall.

She wanted to be recognized for her contributions to the field of forensic anthropology, and at some point, to find another mate and have a child. Or children. Seeking a new job was important, however, her biggest desire was to be part of a typical family, the kind she never had as a child. Too many foster homes to count then adopted. Security for a few years until her illness and the death of the couple's child, a time in her life she preferred not to dwell upon.

Seated at the only chair in the tent, Grace ran a hand over her face. She'd almost made it, but then a car crash took her husband's life, injured her, and she lost the baby she carried. Tears pooled in her eyes.

Kristy Miller, the youngest crew member, called, "Grace, come see what I found."

She swiped at her cheeks, squared her shoulders, and headed to Secondo, the second dig where Kristy worked. Marcus had named the sites using Latin ordinal numbers.

"Look, a skull." Kristy pointed. "A clavicle and a femur."

"You've done a great job. Carry on exposing the rest of the skeleton." Grace squatted. "I trust you."

The student beamed. "Thanks, prof." She brushed dirt away from the top of the skull, revealing a series of line fractures. "Looks like he died a violent death."

"Don't be too quick to reach a conclusion. We need to examine the whole skeleton before we can make any determination. Take your time. We're in no rush." Grace stood. "Let me know when you've uncovered more bones." She was curious to see how much of this skeleton they'd find.

Marcus supervised Susan and Charles, the other two crew members, digging in the Primus site about fifteen meters away. Grace approached them. "Any more bones?"

"No." Susan straightened. "Can we work someplace else now?"

"I want to make sure we've uncovered all the site

has to offer."

"What does it matter?"

Susan's derogatory tone ate at Grace's patience. "Forensically, it matters." She turned to walk away then said over her shoulder, "Marcus, come to the tent, please."

He followed her. "What's up?"

"I noticed Susan has been distracted lately. Do you know what's wrong?"

"She and Charles argued. He, um, hinted he had a girlfriend at home."

Grace knew she might have to deal with relationship issues when she'd taken on this assignment mentoring four young adults working closely together and living in the same house. "I don't want her personal problems interfering with our work. Send her to help Kristy for now. I'll talk to her after a while."

An hour later as Grace typed the last entry in her report, Kristy called her again. She hurried to the site.

"We've uncovered more bones. They are mixed up. I found a humerus next to a tibia and the skull is missing the lower mandible. However, I've determined by the brow ridge, that he's possibly male." Kristy pointed to the skull with the handle of her small trowel.

"I concur," added Susan.

Grace noted the prominent ridge. "You're right. But as with the other two skeletons, once we can examine the sciatic arch, we can be more certain. Carry on." She returned to the tent and closed her laptop. Until the bones were officially dated at Oxford, her expertise in dating bones for forensic purposes in contemporary deaths was of no use here, and it didn't matter. The many excavations since 1860 had provided details for the varied civilizations who had lived in the area.

The two digs were only meters apart along the lake shore. It was conceivable the bones were from the same period and maybe had shared a grave at one time. Grace headed back to Primus where Charles was carefully brushing off dirt around an object while Marcus took pictures. "What did you find?"

"A piece of pottery." The small brush in Charles's large hand looked like a toy.

"Yes. A large, curved piece." Marcus carefully removed the item. "A shard, about ten centimeters by, um, six." He stood and handed the find to Grace.

"I'll examine it under the microscope. Good job, guys."

"Just in time. Look." Charles scooted back from the hole. "Water is seeping in."

"I'm not surprised. Actually, I expected it sooner. The water table is high this close to the lake."

Gradually, the precisely cut sides of the meter-deep hole collapsed. Secundus was two meters further away from the lake, but Grace called to the women. "Watch for any sign of water entering the dig. Primus has been reclaimed."

She carried the precious find to the tent, dipped it in a bowl of clean water, and washed off the remaining dirt. Once dried, she examined it under the battery-powered table magnifying lamp. Her suspicions confirmed, Grace set the pottery on a small tray. Time to share the news with the crew. She walked toward Secundus and called the students who raised their heads and stood.

Knowing she wouldn't be working with this group

much longer, she eyed them as they approached. Kristy led the pack. The humidity caused her dyed blonde hair to frizz around her chubby face, but she didn't seem to care. She gave Grace a wide grin, apparently still basking in her earlier praise.

Susan Thanh, slim, and a few inches taller than Grace, often made the group chuckle when she described her Vietnamese parents' reactions to the oddities of life in England. They'd only been in the country five years and were slow to adapt.

Large, beefy, and baldheaded, Charles Fulbright-Pool did not resemble the typical student. He looked as if he should be a wrestler, but he was smart and intuitive. And Marcus. As Grace's righthand man, she'd be lost without him. When her year at Oxford ended, she'd miss the crew.

He stopped near her and set his hands on his hips. "What gives, prof?"

With the pottery piece displayed on a small tray, she held it out to the group. "This is not Roman. My preliminary examination revealed scored linear patterns on the simple bowl or jar. The bluish clay is unglazed, probably fired in an open fire." She passed the tray to Marcus. "I can't make any determination by the color as we don't know where they procured the clay, but if you look closely, you can see outlines of seeds and grasses." She waited until all had a chance to view the piece.

"If not Roman, what do you think it is?" Susan, the only member to wear gloves while excavating, had removed them and handed the tray back to Grace.

"It reminds me of cremation urns I've seen in the Ashmolean Museum at Oxford. This piece might be close to the rim of the urn. The curve is profound. And I'd give a tentative date of early Saxon, as in 600 AD."

Kristy tried to tuck a few curls behind her ear. "What does that mean for us, our work here? And the skeletal remains?"

"Right." Susan muttered a Vietnamese phrase, then added, "We're here because the original piece of pottery was dated from the Roman period."

"Remember the history of this area we studied before we left Oxford, the previous excavations, and the gravel works? Dr. Wilson approved the project because of that history. We're as likely to find items from the Roman period as we are any of the other civilizations who lived here. According to the latest geophysical survey, there are anomalies in the area east of this lake. She and I decided to set up here for two reasons. First, to give you more hands-on experience. Second, to assure Sir Barrette he could install a dock anywhere along this section without finding artifacts or bones that would hinder his projects again. Dr. Wilson and I were right."

She looked at each student in turn and then asked, "Considering what we've found, what are your thoughts about this site?"

"The only artifact is the piece of pottery which you don't recognize as Roman." Kristy was the first to speak. Usually, Susan was way ahead of her.

Arms crossed against his broad chest, Charles said, "The graves don't resemble any Roman ones I've seen before."

"Given the history of the site, we shouldn't be surprised we found no traditional burials." Level-headed Marcus as always made a logical statement.

"And remember, locating human remains here is highly unusual."

"Marcus is correct. Maybe that's another reason Dr. Wilson wants us to continue." Grace set the small tray on the table. "Let's—"

"There's something I don't understand." Susan toyed with the gloves in her hand. "The bones we found don't look like they've been in a moist environment for hundreds of years."

"When were these lakes formed?" Grace had always thought Susan didn't complete all the assigned readings.

"Sometime after the gravel excavations stopped, fifty years ago?" Charles rolled his eyes.

"Right. And what kind of environment were they in before that?"

"Well-drained earth, similar to the in the big Salmonsbury Camp area."

"Charles, you did your homework. Good." Grace looked directly at Susan who narrowed her eyes and pursed her lips.

Fifteen seconds later, she tilted her chin. "Dr. Gentry, what are we going to do now?"

"I appreciate everyone's input. Naturally, the pottery and bones will be dated back at Oxford with more sophisticated equipment than my eyes."

Charles and Susan started to speak at once. He gestured for Susan to continue. "Does this mean we'll have to stop working here?"

"Yeah." Charles huffed. "And will this affect our marks for this term? We want to get our money's worth for this course."

"No need to worry at this point. I'll let Dr. Wilson

know, and she'll confer with her colleagues. In the meantime, we carry on working. Okay?"

All but Marcus slouched away. "Hey, this might not be a Roman site, but it is a grave site, nonetheless."

"True. The bones will be treated with the utmost respect. Until I hear back from Dr. Wilson, please study the topography map and decide where we can begin another dig. I want to keep Kristy in charge of Secundus."

"Thanks for allowing me to choose a site." Marcus unearthed the map from the back table.

Mumbled, angry voices caught Grace's attention. Charles and Susan were huddled together while Kristy continued working on the bones. The knowledge they might have to wrap up the excavation soon had probably set nerves on edge. Grace was surprised at Charles's earlier question. She knew nothing of the students' financial situations and wanted to keep it that way.

Approaching the site, she asked, "Are you two all right?"

They immediately hushed and stepped apart.

"Susan says you should have known this wasn't Roman. She knew right away."

"Really?" Grace's eyebrows shot up. "Why didn't you say something? An excavation is always a collaborative endeavor."

She huffed and looked away.

"Share your reasoning with us."

Susan shrugged. "Well, the bones were, um, mixed up, and I just didn't think they were Roman."

A smirk touched Charles's face. "We worked side by side and you never hinted at any problem."

"It was more of a guess than anything." Dark eyes downcast and a pout on her lips, Susan dug the toe of her boot into the gravel.

"We base our conclusions on evidence, not on guesswork." Grace held back additional criticism of Susan. "In the future, if anyone has a concern, please speak up. Charles, you stay here and help Kristy. Marcus, continue to identify another area to dig." She turned toward the tent, then stopped and pivoted. "And before anyone states the obvious, yes, we will continue to excavate this site until Dr. Wilson tells us to quit. Susan, come with me, please."

Back inside the tent, Grace drew in a quick breath. She hated confrontation, but she'd had enough of the student's attitude. "I want you to help me tag the most recent bones we found."

"Really? I thought you were going to, um, give me a lecture."

"Do you think you deserve it?"

Writing numerals on a tag, Susan kept her head lowered. "Yeah. Sorry for being disrespectful and questioning your judgment."

"You're a good student. Exemplary work so far." Grace tied a tag to a humerus. "Keep your personal issues separate from our tasks at the dig site."

Susan sniggered. "Is it that obvious?" She crossed her arms. "Charles is…is an idiot."

Not about to take sides, Grace straightened several vertebrae. "We don't know how much longer we'll be here in Bourton. We must focus on our job and not on our—"

"Love life?"

Grace chuckled. "Exactly. Can you and Charles

call a truce?"

"Certainly." Susan harrumphed. "Now I won't have to tell my parents about my non-Vietnamese boyfriend."

With the last bone tagged, Grace jutted her chin toward the tent flap. "Thanks for your help. Go help Marcus find the next place to dig."

Susan opened the flap and then turned. "Thank you, Dr. Gentry. Thank you for not embarrassing me in front of my peers."

Pleased with what she considered an appropriate handling of the situation, Grace promptly sagged into the chair. Dealing with these students who lived and worked in such close quarters sure was harder than she'd imagined.

A few deep breaths later, she stood and almost knocked a bucket off the table. Bucket. Bucket list. The image of Logan, the large enthusiastic man wandered into her mind.

Why did his mother have a bucket list? Was she ill? Grace would probably never know. Logan might have been all-mouth and not interested in their dig at all. But despite his arrogant manner, she hoped he'd visit the site.

CHAPTER 3

After breakfast the next morning, Mother and Reggie sat at the large table in the conservatory playing board games. Later in the morning, they were going to the Model Village. Mother remembered visiting when she was a child and was anxious to see if it was the same.

Following Marcus's directions, Logan set out at a brisk pace and soon reached the graveled parking area between the two lakes. A white van with a small decal on the door identifying it as belonging to the University of Oxford confirmed he'd reached the correct place. He'd checked online reports of the archeological digs done previously at Salmonsbury Camp Hillfort and was impressed by the many interesting finds. Eager to see what Grace and her team had found, Logan hurried to the tent in the distance partially hidden behind bushes. People walking the trail around the west shore of the lake to his left might not even notice it.

Marcus and the dark-haired female team member stood at the line of trees and shrubs beside that lake and their wild gestures seemed to indicate they were arguing.

Logan didn't see anyone else about and approached the couple. "Hey, Marcus."

The man turned to Logan. "Good morning." Then he pointed beyond the tent. "Susan, we have work to do. Please continue excavating Tertius."

"Tertius?"

"Our third site." Marcus ran his fingers through his long curls and chuckled. "Grace asked me to give them names. I'll check with her to see if I can show you around."

"Thanks." Hands in his pockets, mouth dry, and heartbeat at a gallop, Logan watched Marcus enter the tent.

Moments later, Grace exited with the student and closed the flap behind her. She eyed Logan up and down. "So, you came. I didn't think you would."

His heart rate returned to normal. No hint she reciprocated his interest. But he had to ask, "Why?"

She shrugged and covered her mouth before she turned away. He was sure she hid a smile. "I can show you around, but then I have to supervise the team as they search for more bones of the third skeleton we found."

"May I see the area and take photos?"

"I suppose, but not of the students without their permission." She led the way to where two of the crew squatted in the hole, brushing away dirt from the bones.

"Kristy, explain to Logan what you and Charles are doing."

The blonde looked up briefly and then continued her task. "We're removing as much dirt as possible without damaging the bones. When several are exposed, we'll move them to a table in the tent where we'll label the bones and examine them carefully to determine sex and age."

"And possible cause of death. He might have suffered a blow." Charles patted the side of his head. "There are fractures in his temporal region. But I also know what happened here years ago, so any damage to bones may have occurred then."

"Interesting. Have you found any artifacts?" Logan shot several pictures of the site.

"We have. Come back to the tent." Grace shoved her hands into her packets. "Can I trust you, Logan?"

"Of course." He lifted the flap, and she proceeded him inside.

"First of all, why do you want to take pictures?"

"Photography is my hobby. I've taken loads of photos of the Roman sites I've visited so far, but I've never been to an active dig before." His new Canon Rebel camera had proven to be worth the money.

"Marcus and Charles found this yesterday, right before water seeped into the Primus dig." She removed a cloth from an object on a small tray. "I'm certain the piece of pottery is from a cremation urn, probably Saxon around 600AD. The striations are very typical of that period. At least two hundred years after the Romans left."

"And the bones? Can you date them?"

"Just by a cursory examination, no. They are old, but they'll be dated back at Oxford. Usually, artifacts found with skeletons as well as how they were buried help us date them. However, this is not—" Her phone buzzed, and she drew it from her pocket. "Sorry, I have to take this, and I can't leave you in here. Please go to Tertius and see what Marcus and Susan are doing."

They left the tent together. Grace hurried toward the parking area and Logan located the third site on a slight elevation.

Marcus grinned as he looked up. "You should feel fortunate Grace allowed you access to our site. You're the only regular civilian to visit."

"I am honored. What are you two doing here?"

"According to the latest geophysical survey, there are anomalies along this slight ridge. We have permission to explore, but only here. Primus revealed bones from two humans we've arranged in the tent, and Kristy is working on more skeletal remains in Secundus. As you can see, we used a grid to divide this area into small sections. Right now, we're removing the top layer of dirt."

Although interested, Logan kept an eye on Grace, and when she started walking back to the excavation site, he said, "Thank you. Um, Grace looks like she received bad news." He knew disappointment when he saw it. Shoulders sagging, head down, taking small steps as if in no hurry to return to the tent. "Do you know what's going on?"

Voice low, Marcus responded, "She applied for a teaching positing at Brandeis University in Massachusetts. Maybe she received bad news."

That might account for her demeanor. "When will she complete her assignment? How long will you be working here?"

"She'll leave us in December, but we hope to have this site wrapped up before then."

By now Grace had joined them. "Do you want to

see the other skeletons we found?" She cleared her throat as if the action would remove the dark tone from her voice.

"Certainly, but before we do, tell me why you're allowed to excavate here. I read online about the archeological history of the area and the gravel excavations that left deep pits which filled with water to create these lakes."

She gave him a bright smile. "You've done your homework. I'm impressed."

Logan opened the tent flap and followed her inside. Her praise was like a gold star for his efforts. He beamed at her.

"Salmonsbury Camp Hillfort is a Scheduled Ancient Monument and several years ago, the authorities determined no more excavations should be carried out here. However, Sir Barrette, who owns this land, is my boss's sister. So, when he found a Roman pottery shard one day, Oxford agreed to send us out."

"Thank you, Sir Barrette." Logan wasn't sure Grace had heard, but then she smiled at him again sending all rational thoughts out of his head.

Although she provided details on the partial skeletons, the information barely registered on his radar. Adult female evidenced by the sciatic arch. Male, eyebrow arch very prominent. Missing his right hand.

A documentary Logan had watched about ancient medical practices jumped into his mind. He blurted out, "Maybe the guy had leprosy."

"What?" Grace set her dainty hands on her almost nonexistent hips.

Brought down to earth, he replied, "Just a thought. Forgive me. I don't know why I said that."

Frowning, she tilted her head. "As good an explanation as anything I've postulated."

His phone buzzed. Why now when Grace's attitude toward him seemed to be thawing? But he checked the text anyway. Reggie reported Mother had fallen and was asking for him. "Sorry, I'm at Mother's beck and call. Can I come back another day?"

"How long are you staying in Bourton?"

"We leave sometime next week. Mother wants to use Bourton as a base to visit other villages she remembers in the Cotswolds." However, to date, she hadn't asked to visit any.

Instead of answering his request to return, Grace smiled again as he lifted the tent flap. Was the smile in response to his staying in the village or his leaving?

CHAPTER 4

Mother's fall resulted in a bruised ego, but nothing physical. She needed Logan's company more for assurance than his medical skills. He stayed close and even played a game of dominoes with her after lunch.

An hour later, her self-confidence had returned, and she shooed him off to the grocery store. Although his birthday was two days away, she wanted to bake him a cake. Now. She had all the ingredients except powdered sugar for the frosting.

After purchasing the necessary item, he crossed the river and headed toward Victoria Street. On a bench close to The Corner Inn sat a woman wearing a pink jacket. Grace? She stared at the ducks paddling in the water, and not to startle her, he stood beside the bench until she noticed him.

"Hi. May I join you?"

A brief smile and she nodded.

The sun retreated behind gray clouds and a chill wind stirred the yellow and red leaves scattered on the grass. The absent sunlight seemed to make her face almost translucent and dulled the sparkle in her eyes.

"I enjoyed my visit today."

She shoved her hands into her pockets and acted as if she didn't hear, but before he repeated his statement, she turned to him. "I'd like you to come again."

"Great. How about tomorrow? Mother is in one of her needy moods today." Grace's invitation acted as a shot of caffeine.

"That will be fine. We unearthed bones from a child mixed in with this last skeleton. I have a question about the femurs you may be able to answer."

"I'd love to help. I—"

"Tell me about your mother. Who is the other woman with her?"

How would Grace know about Reggie? He had no problem talking about his mother but didn't think a relative stranger would be interested. It might be her way of keeping him from prying into her life. "Mom's name is Irene, and her good friend Regina is traveling with us."

"I had a brief conversation with them at church Sunday. It's hard to miss two women with American accents. They were besieged by congregants."

Church, yeah. Before Logan had dropped them off, he had to remind Mother several times he was not interested.

"Hope you don't mind me asking, why does Irene have a bucket list?"

"She'd be the first one to tell you. Mother was diagnosed with early onset Alzheimer's a year ago."

"I'm sorry. That's a devasting disease. Especially for someone so…. How old is she?"

"Only fifty-seven. She's handling the diagnosis like the trouper she is. As a nurse, she recognized the symptoms. She's always been headstrong and stubborn and a few months ago she asked me, as her only child, to help her complete her bucket list."

"While she can still remember the things she wants to do."

"Exactly. I, uh, have taken a leave of absence from my practice so our trip is giving me something to occupy my time and to help her. She's been such a support to me, and this is a small way I can repay her."

The gentle rippling of the river and the chirping of numerous sparrows on the branches above enhanced their silence. Logan wondered if Grace had heard enough and he was ready to ask about her job when she placed her small hand on his forearm and asked, "What are some things on her list?"

"Back home she wanted to visit her alma mater in Tennessee, old college friends, the house where she was born and lived until she married." He didn't add details about the marriage that ended painfully for Mother and Logan. "And here in the UK, we've been to Edinburgh to the Military Tattoo—"

"But that was back in August."

"Right. We attended the last performance. We've been in the UK a while, but Mother has a long list."

Grace let out a giggle which made her sound like a child.

His heart somersaulted. For whatever reason he couldn't describe, the need to protect her resurfaced. She seemed so vulnerable, small, and... Shaking off those disquieting feelings, he continued. "Mother always wanted to stay in a castle, so we spent several nights at Melville Castle, just south of Edinburgh. Oh, my, she loved that." His turn to chuckle. "You should see our luggage. Mother brought all kinds of clothes, and she dressed up each evening for dinner. You'd think she was royalty."

"Sounds as if she enjoyed that visit."

"She did. I have a photo of her posing on the spiral staircase as if she owned the place." He shook his head recalling her swagger. "Here in England, we've visited the Yorkshire Dales, the Lake District, and now Bourton-on-the-Water."

"Why here? There are many cute villages in the Cotswolds."

"Her grandfather was stationed near here during World War Two and often came back to visit friends he'd made at that time. He'd bring Dennis his son, my grandfather, who made lasting friendships, too. To keep the tradition alive, Dennis brought his young family on vacations here. According to Mother, those holidays were some of the best times of her childhood. One of her Dad's friends had a daughter her age, and they explored the village, fished in the river, and wandered the countryside unabandoned."

Grace sighed. "Sounds like a magical time."

Accompanying that sigh was an impression Logan got that she'd experienced no such holidays in her childhood. This might not be the appropriate time to inquire.

"Where are you going from here?"

"London. Mother has visited before, but she's never been to Harrods."

"I've been in England nearly a year already and haven't spent any time in the big city."

"If there weren't Roman ruins there, I would be dreading the visit, but Mom has—"

Grace's phone buzzed. She nabbed it immediately and checked the screen.

Seated at an angle, he noticed her face pale as she stood.

"Marcus has been attacked at the site. The…the guy tried to destroy the bones." She stepped backward and hesitated as if she didn't know which way to go.

"I have a car. I can take you." Logan took her arm and tried to draw her toward Victoria Street.

"No. Thanks. I know a shortcut along a footpath." She ran across the bridge and headed east on High Street.

Whether Grace wanted his help or not, he was going to the site. First, he ran to the cottage, dropped the package of powdered sugar on the table and while he gave Mother a quick rundown of his plan, he grabbed the car keys. Fingers fumbling, he had to enter the lock code on the garage door twice before it clicked open. He yanked the doors wide, climbed into the vehicle, and tore out of the driveway.

He arrived seconds after Grace reached the graveled parking area. He was surprised she wasn't out of breath. She must be fit. He jogged with her to the tent where the crew crowded around Marcus.

He sat in a chair outside the tent, holding tissues to his bloody nose.

"Are you all right?" Grace patted the man's shoulder. "Here's Logan. He's a doctor."

"I'm fine." Marcus withdrew another wad of tissues from the box Kristy held. "The chap lunged at me, but I dodged, and he just hit the side of my nose.

Then he made a beeline to one skeleton and swiped the bones off the table, but before he could stomp on them, I kicked out at his knee and yelled for help. Charles chased him away."

"He was fast. Sorry, I couldn't nab him." Charles hiked a shoulder.

Logan made a quick assessment of Marcus's injury. The way he pinched his nostrils meant no serious damage. "Do we call the police? What's the protocol for someone vandalizing an excavation site?'

"No police. Yet." Grace opened the tent flap. "I need to see what damage was done."

"Marcus, describe the man." Grace gave Logan a wary look. "In case you want to get the authorities involved."

"He had a scarf wrapped around his neck which covered the bottom of his face, but I could tell he was white. Young. Maybe a beard. Brown hair." He dabbed at his nose which appeared to have stopped bleeding. "Oh, and a scar on his hand. Looked like a burn scar."

"I agree. He was average build, average height." Charles nodded, then added, "And interesting trainers. I noticed the colorful soles as he ran away."

"Trainers?"

"You call them sneakers."

"Helpful details to pass on to the cops." Logan noted Grace had entered the tent. He followed, as did the crew.

"What does the man have against these ancient remains? His actions seem so senseless." She picked up the bones one by one and set them back on the table. "Charles and Susan, since this is the female from the Primus site you worked on, please place the bones in anatomical order."

When they completed the task, Grace asked, "Are any bones missing?"

"No," Susan replied.

"Good. And all the male's bones we excavated are here, except for his right hand, of course. No equipment is missing either." Grace shook her head. "So, what was he after?"

"Marcus, your quick action might have thwarted his plan. Good job. And you, too Charles."

"I agree with Logan." Grace jutted her chin toward the exit. "Please, return to your dig sites. I'll make the necessary notifications."

"Where is the nearest police station?"

"In Stow-on-the-Wold, but first, I'll notify my supervisor. Thanks for your support. Maybe you can return tomorrow to examine the child's bones we found."

"Certainly. Are you sure I can't help with anything else?"

Grace removed the band holding her ponytail in place and ran her fingers through her hair. "No, but I look forward to seeing you tomorrow."

Logan tucked a business card into her hand. "Here's my cell number. Call if you need me. Take care." He walked away and then turned. Grace watched him leave. She gave him a sweet smile.

If he wasn't driving, he'd click his heels together and then strut all the way home.

His jubilance changed to annoyance tinged with curiosity when he pulled into Victoria Street. The man wearing a familiar green jacket dashed down Bow Street.

CHAPTER 5

The cool air inside the tent nipped at Grace's fingers as she placed the last of the male's skeletal remains in the specifically designed container. Surrounded by cushioning and breathable material, the bones would be supported and safe from mold growth or breakage. Or another wild intruder's visit. Marcus had driven the van to the dig site and carried the containers into the tent after Grace had conferred with Peggy. "Keep the remains safe at all costs." *Yes, ma'am.*

With the two excavated skeletons taken care of, Grace pondered what to do about the bones still in Secundus. The dig had proven difficult as at least two individuals were involved, along with animal bones, probably sheep. Although Kristy and Charles had worked feverishly, Grace was hesitant to remove any bones until all had been revealed.

Faced with the task of keeping the latest find secure, too, Grace closed the second container then left the tent and approached Marcus and Susan. "I want you to help at Secundus. We need to safeguard those bones before we leave for the evening. And I checked the weather. A good chance of rain is predicted for tomorrow. We know from experience the pop-up canopy might not be sufficient cover to keep the dig dry. Dr. Wilson insists we complete this excavation. Someone in real time doesn't want us here. Maybe these bones will tell us why."

They weren't equipped to dig at night. Grace hoped the four crew members would uncover all the bones and artifacts in Secundus before they had to quit. While watching them work, a police officer approached, and Grace hurried to meet her.

"I'm Constable Lambert. Are you Dr. Gentry?"

"Yes." She drew the constable toward the tent and relayed all relevant details including the description of the intruder Marcus had shared.

"Nothing was taken?"

"Correct."

"May I enter the tent?"

"Of course." Grace opened the flap.

Lambert took notes on the contents. "Are those large containers for the bones?"

"Yes. We'll store the skeletal remains in our van where they should be safe."

"Good idea. I'll provide the man's description to my sergeant, check around the village for other acts of vandalism, and report back if I have any news." Lambert shoved her notepad into her pocket. "The incident doesn't sound like some teenager trying to lay his hands on bones for a Halloween prank."

"Not at all. If Marcus hadn't intervened, the man would have crushed the bones underfoot."

"There's not much else I can do since nothing was taken and your co-worker's injury was mild. That is unless he wants to level charges."

"No, he doesn't. Thanks for coming out." Fully aware of how much daylight they had left, Grace hurried back to Secundus. Even a vee-formation of honking geese overhead didn't distract her as they had done when the team first arrived.

Site log in hand, Marcus pointed to the area where the others worked. "More bones of a child. I think we've almost uncovered the whole skeleton."

"What haven't you found yet?"

"A few vertebrae and most of the carpals and tarsals."

"Noting how tiny the fibula is, the toes and fingers will be easy to miss." Susan reached for her water bottle on the rim of the dig and took a sip. "We should have a screen to sift the soil."

"I agree, however, even if we had one, we don't have time to use it today." Grace had wanted to include more equipment, but her request had been axed by the "guardian" of the equipment room. He'd probably never been to a dig site before and…. Grace shook off the negative thoughts. "How about the adult, Kristy?"

"The bones are on top of each other. This burial site was compromised long ago." Kristy continued working. "And here we have a metacarpal. I'd say sheep, maybe." She held up the small bone.

Just what they needed. More animals mixed in with the human remains. "I'm making an executive decision: We will remove the bones we've uncovered so far and get them into bins for safe storage. Marcus, come help me, please." She strode into the tent and picked up three metal trays. "Use one for the animal bones. At this point, it won't matter if we mix them up. One for the child and the other one for the adult."

"Will do." Trays in hand, he left the tent.

Grace documented her decision in her report. Better to save what they could in case the intruder returned, or the site was further compromised by rain or rising lake levels.

Fifteen minutes later, Marcus returned with the child's bones on the tray. "A bit of news. Charles just unearthed the femur and tibia of an adult. The bones are charred."

"That's interesting. Only those two?"

"So far. We're making good progress. It's just tight with all four of us working in the same hole."

"That's why I haven't volunteered my services. Tell the team to be extra careful. Charred bones are especially fragile."

Alone with the child's remains and loath to begin her examination, Grace reflected on the charring. If only a femur and tibia were involved, then the burning had nothing to do with the burial. And no other charred bones had been found. A thorough examination of all the bones back at the university labs would answer many of her questions.

Grace attempted to place the small bones in anatomical order on the table. Although her accident occurred five years ago and she was only six months pregnant at the time, examining skeletal remains of a child always rekindled her grief. The small bones still had the power to remind her of what she'd lost. But in this case, she knew someone who was an expert, a pediatric surgeon.

She unearthed Logan's card from her pocket and palmed her phone. Did she need his help or did she want to see him again? He talked loudly—which might be for her benefit—and he was large, in physique and ego, but his concern for his mother touched a spot in her heart. Irene must be a wonderful person to command such love and devotion from her son.

Grace picked up a femur which had an odd, bowed shape. Yes, she needed Logan's expertise. She dialed his number.

He answered right away. "Logan Quinn."

"Um, this is Grace. From the excavation," she added in case he didn't remember. "Would you like to come tomorrow to examine the child's skeleton I mentioned?"

"I'd love to, but Mother has requested a trip to Broadway and other villages in the morning. I can come after lunch if she doesn't add to her list of places to visit."

"That will be fine." She ended the call and huffed out a breath. She'd have to wait. Instead of placing the bones on the table, she carefully nestled them in a storage container.

For a brief moment, she wished she could join Logan and Irene on their ride.

CHAPTER 6

Photographs of the Cotswold countryside, even those taken with a fancy camera, didn't do it justice. Most fields were still green and early morning mist hung in the low valleys. Raindrops from the overnight showers glistened on the vegetation. Logan felt like he was driving through a fairytale land.

He used the rearview mirror to look at Reggie in the backseat. "Thanks for reminding me to order tickets for the Broadway Tower online. I completely forgot."

"You're welcome. I've never seen such wonderful scenery before."

"I love it, too. Thanks for driving, son."

Knowing ahead of time Mother wanted to visit villages in the Cotswolds, he'd studied a map of the area in preparation for any of her quirky requests concerning places she remembered from when she was a kid. Although she requested this trip and time with her was precious, he had chomped at the bit to get back to Bourton. Then he felt guilty when she glowed with happiness and spent hours retelling exploits from her childhood.

As they walked around the unusual edifice and explored the museum inside, Mother recalled the time she and her friend Lorraine, had raced up the staircases to the roof access way ahead of her parents. By the time her father reached the top, the girls were leaning over the railings. He reprimanded them and threatened no more jaunts if they misbehaved again. While she reminisced, Logan took numerous pictures of the tower and the countryside and included Mother when she cooperated.

He'd heard some of her stories before, but others were news to him. No wonder this area was a priority on her bucket list. It held many wonderful memories for her. One of which was having lunch in Stow-on-the-Wold at The Porch House, supposedly England's oldest inn. During the meal, Mother regaled him with another escapade from the time she dined there with her parents. She and Lorraine had been excused from the table while the adults lingered over dessert. Mother, the instigator it seemed, convinced Lorraine to climb the twisted, crooked staircase. They knocked on several doors and might have run away unscathed if a guest hadn't opened his door and hollered at them.

The trip had exhausted Mother, and for the remainder of the afternoon, she planned on nothing more exciting than crocheting. A good thing Reggie also had something to keep her hands busy. That woman was a saint. She was writing an autobiography on her laptop, but always kept a wary eye on Irene.

After assuring all was well at the cottage, Logan set off on foot for the dig site. The tent and canopies drew him like magnets. His pulse raced, and not from the long walk. Dainty Dr. Grace had caught his attention the moment he'd seen her. He'd always mocked peers who claimed to fall in love instantly, that it was the hormones talking, but now he'd succumbed, he was sure it was more substantial than mere physical attraction. He wanted nothing more than to make her happy.

Marcus hailed him to the far canopy.

Logan tromped over the soggy gravel to the site. "Did

the rain do any damage?"

"Not much. We'd secured all the bones before we left for the night. Took them with us. We have some water collection in Secundus, but Kristy and Charles are working there anyway. Susan and I are making progress in Tertius."

"Where's Grace?"

"In the tent." Marcus squatted and scooped out a shovelful of damp gravel.

Hands tucked into his pockets, Logan walked toward the tent. He felt as if he were going to ask a girl to the prom. Palms sweating, gut muscles jittery. *Calm, down, Logan.* He opened the flap. "Good afternoon."

She welcomed him with a smile. Usually, the simple act transformed her face, but she had circles under her eyes as if she hadn't slept well.

"Hi. Did Irene have a good time today?"

"Yes, but the excitement wore her out. How about you? Have you been busy?"

"You'll notice the adult skeletal remains are not here. They're in storage bins in the van. We don't want an intruder to have access to them."

"Marcus told me." He pointed to the bones she'd displayed on a white cloth. "The child, you mentioned?"

"Yes. Quite a few bones are missing. Some vertebrae and ribs, the left scapula. We only have the frontal skull bone. But the femurs puzzle me. I've studied them over and over and I can't decide why they're bowed."

Logan bent and visually examined the bones, first a femur then the fibula. "No metacarpals or metatarsals?"

"No. We didn't bring a screen to sift the soil and we were in a hurry yesterday to pack up what we'd found. Kristy and Charles are still excavating."

He picked up a humerus, closed his eyes, and ran his fingers along the small bone. The child couldn't have been older than five. He felt a slight ridge and opened his eyes. "Can I use your magnifying lamp?"

"Sure. It's battery powered." She turned it on.

Carefully holding the bone under the glass, he examined the almost invisible ridge. Yes, there it was. "Look here."

Grace leaned in beside him. "Is that remodeling?"

"I believe so. The child must have suffered the fracture several years before death. I'll take a guess and say the arm was splinted while it healed. Is that usual for the Roman or Anglo-Saxon timeframe?"

"I have seen it before, but not often. Fractures usually healed at an angle." She moved away from the table, her shoulders slumped. "I can't believe I missed it."

"The only reason I checked is because I believe this child suffered from rickets."

"Rickets?"

"Yes. The bowed femurs are a sure sign as are the slightly enlarged ends of the long bones, and the boxy shape of the brow."

"I did notice those anomalies."

"Yeah. During life, the disease softens the growth plates. Bones are easily broken or fractured. There are stress fractures in one humerus and one femur."

"Why do you know so much about rickets?"

"I spent six months with Doctors Without Borders. We worked in Uganda, in Central Africa. Rickets is not a common malady in most countries, but in children who have dark skin, vitamin D absorption can be minimized, thus causing rickets. A lack of calcium in the diet is also a contributing factor."

"That's interesting. I wonder why this child? Even if the family didn't have access to cow's milk, goat's milk is high in calcium."

"Maybe she didn't like milk."

"We'll never know, but despite having rickets, the child was well taken care of. Someone cared enough to splint her arm."

"Was she buried alone?"

Grace shook her head and backed up a few steps.

"What's the matter? You have found children before, right?"

She drew in a breath. "Of course, but every so often, finding a child gets to me."

The maternal instinct maybe, but he knew better than to broach the subject at the moment. "When I operate on a child, I have to steel myself against the emotions that surface. I focus on the surgery and what the kid needs to be healthy again."

Enough words. He tentatively placed his hand on her shoulder, and she didn't pull away. Change the subject. "Um, do you and the crew work seven days a week?"

"No. Not unless we have time constraints at the dig site. Here, we have a roster and take off different days. Other than doing laundry, I like to stroll around Bourton or hike to another village. It's so peaceful in the countryside."

"Did you grow up in a city?"

She hung her head. "I did. Several in fact, but let's get back to the bones." Shoulders squared, she turned off the magnifying lamp.

Touchy subject. But with time, he would ask more about her childhood. "Do you think the child was buried at the same time as the adults you found?"

"Probably. Her bones are mixed in with another male. His remains are in a tub at the dig. This might have been a family burial site." She tenderly stroked the bones, then picked up the partial skull. "I'd like to identify the sex of the child, but the only evidence I can find is the smoothness of the bones. What do you think?'

"I don't know enough about the differences at this young age. But I think female. Even with the abnormality, I can see the slope of the brow ridge is very gentle."

"I agree." She clasped her stomach as if in pain.

"Hey, you're not getting sick are you?"

Shaking her head, she left the tent and walked away.

He followed her toward the parking area. "What's wrong?"

"I'm sorry. I just couldn't be in there with the child's remains any longer."

The sadness in her voice stabbed at his heart. He drew her behind a clump of bushes out of sight of the crew and wrapped his arms around her. She was so small and delicate. To his amazement, she rested her head against his chest.

She remained that way as she spoke, "Five years ago, my husband and I were in a car wreck. A large pickup hit the passenger side and he died instantly. I was pinned in the wreckage for two hours. I didn't have any broken bones, but I lost my baby. My little girl died in my womb."

Her story answered so many questions, but he had the good sense not to comment. He just held her and rested his head on hers.

When he felt the tenseness ease in her body, he said, "I'm so sorry."

Minutes trickled by. Minutes he relished with her in his arms.

Then she backed away. "Thanks for listening. It's been a long time since I felt comfortable enough with someone to share my story."

"I'm honored."

Her phone buzzed.

Darn. He knew she had to read the text.

"It's Marcus. They've found bones in Tertius. I have to go."

"See you tomorrow?"

"Sure." She set off but stopped. "I mean it. Thank you for being here at the right time."

For once he'd offered what a woman needed without expecting anything in return.

CHAPTER 7

Heavy rain the next day kept the crew home. They all had reports to write, and Grace especially had tons of paperwork to complete. Her time at Oxford was drawing to a close, as was the supervision of the students with her on this excavation. Peggy's reason for granting her brother's request to send a crew to Bourton had panned out. They were gaining much-needed field experience and hands-on training.

All the bones were secure in the university van in special containers. If the thug who attempted to destroy some of the bones wanted to mess with the dig site, the boss said not to worry. Just keep the bones they already had, whether they were Roman or Anglo-Saxon or not, and deliver them to the university labs after the exercise concluded. Although the canopies over each site might keep direct rain away, the crew had dug drainage channels so as little water as possible would enter the area.

At the time of the team's arrival, the nearby Inn had no vacancies. Grace had rented a three-bedroom house on Sherborne Street and the students either cooked for themselves or frequented the many village restaurants or cafes. Grace was in the mood for tomato soup and a grilled cheese sandwich, one of the few memories she had of her childhood that brought a smile to her face. She donned her boots and rain jacket and walked to the center of the village.

When she neared the small grocery store, Logan exited with a bag under his arm. Not sure about her appearance—did she even comb her hair this morning?—she wanted to turn away, but he spied her and his face lit up with a grin. She swallowed hard and faced him.

He drew her into the store. "A good day to sit by the fire and sip your favorite drink."

"I agree, but we are low on food, and I've been elected to shop today."

"I suppose you won't be working on the site."

"No. Maybe tomorrow if the mud isn't a hindrance."

"Mother wants a ham sandwich for lunch and breakfast for supper tonight. Reggie will help her cook, especially the biscuits. Would you like to join us?" He removed his cap and ran his fingers through his damp grayish-blond hair.

The man had wavy hair, and here she was with dead straight locks that wouldn't hold a curl if clued in place. "That would be lovely. Thanks. Can I bring anything?"

"Nope. If it's still raining, I can come and get you."

"No worries. I've been rained on before and survived. Where are you staying?"

"We're in Cloisters Cottage, corner of Victoria Street and Chardwar Gardens, close to Smith's Café. That away." He pointed over his shoulder. "How about six? Mother likes to eat early."

"See you then." She headed into the grocery store and purchased ingredients to make soup and sandwiches for the crew. Her delight in her plans for lunch was almost overcome by her eagerness to eat the evening meal with Logan and Irene. It had been a while since she'd been in the company where they all spoke with an American accent. And besides, she liked Irene at first sight.

The soup and sandwiches were a hit with the crew. Grace retired to her room and worked all afternoon. Fingers tired from all the typing, she hastily showered and changed into slacks instead of jeans and hauled out her only blouse with any claim to fashion. A white chiffon with a lacey jabot. Not her usual attire, so when Marcus and Kristie saw her in the living room ready to leave, they both whistled and Marcus raised his eyebrows and said, "Fancy duds, Dr. Grace. Who's the lucky guy?"

Heat filled her cheeks, but she only responded with, "The rain has stopped. Be ready for a full day tomorrow." She opened the door, then added, "I have a dinner invitation. See you later."

"No need to hurry back on our account." He closed the door behind her.

By now her face was on fire. She walked to the cottage, her jacket zipped up against the cool evening air. She hoped the chilly wind would return her complexion to normal by the time she reached her destination. The occasional dog bark accompanied the slap of her boots on the pavement, and pleasant aromas wafted out of the café on the corner.

The outside light of Cloisters beckoned Grace. She rang the bell and instantly Logan opened the door.

"Welcome. Let me take your coat."

She slipped the garment off her arms and allowed him to usher her through the kitchen to the living room. The flickering glow from the fire added to the room's cozy warmth. Grace felt at home right away. Although she understood the chemical reaction taking place in her brain—the release of dopamine that produced a state of euphoria and caused her heart rate to increase—she could have sunk onto the sofa and stayed there forever.

Logan introduced Irene and Reggie. Reggie said little, but Irene set her arm around Grace's shoulders and squeezed. "It's so good to meet you. Logan has told us all about you and your excavations. Come, sit next to me, Grace, my dear."

Once the ladies were seated at the large table in the conservatory, Logan carried in loaded serving dishes. During the meal of scrambled eggs, bacon, biscuits, and gravy, Irene asked Grace many questions but seldom gave her time to answer. Which suited her just fine. Sharing her background never came easy.

Setting her empty plate aside, Irene asked, "Now, my dear, I can't place your accent. Not too southern, but not east or west coast either."

This time, Irene waited for a reply. "I was born in Florida, spent years in foster care then I was adopted at age five. We moved around a lot and ended up in Oklahoma." The pain eating at her core must have shown on her face because Irene placed her hand on Grace's arm.

"Oh, my dear, no need to continue." She cleared her throat. "Where will you go once your assignment at Oxford is over?"

She shrugged. "I don't know. I'm waiting to hear about a job I applied for in Texas."

Logan's eyebrows shot up, but he kept his eyes on his mother.

Irene didn't respond. She patted her hair nutbrown hair and looked at Logan. "Where's my hat, Logan?"

"It's okay Mother, your hat is on the rack by the door. Come, let's move to the living room. Even with the underfloor heating, it's getting cool out here. I'll add more wood to the fire."

"Okay, son." Irene allowed him to guide her to one of the sofas.

Reggie closed the glass doors to the conservatory. "I'll get the dessert ready. Would you like tea or coffee, Grace?"

"Tea, please." She sat on the sofa opposite Irene and Logan. He held his mother's hand, concern etched on his brow.

Grace caught his attention and whispered, "I think it's time for me to go."

He shook his head. "At least stay for tea and cake."

Reggie carried in a tea tray and placed it on the coffee table. She sat beside Grace and passed out plates heavy with slices of thick chocolate cake, then poured the tea and set a cup in front of Grace before handing two cups to Logan.

Grace noticed Reggie had already added the milk. She'd gotten used to drinking tea that way and even enjoyed it.

"Who made this cake? It's delicious." Irene licked

frosting off her lips.

"You did, honey. It's for Logan's birthday." Reggie forked a piece of cake into her mouth.

"But we don't have any candles."

"That's okay, Mom. I don't want candles. I appreciate the cake and the company." He held up his cup in a salute to Grace.

While sipping tea and devouring her slice of cake, Irene stared at Grace as if she didn't recognize her. "Logan, son, you didn't tell me we had company."

"Finish your tea, Mother, then I think it's time for a nice warm bath before bed."

"I agree." Irene set down her cup and plate on the table and rose, brushing crumbs off her sweater. "Goodnight everyone."

Logan eased off the sofa, kissed Irene on the forehead then hugged her. "Do you feel up to climbing all the stairs to the third floor? Maybe take a shower instead."

"You said bath, and that's what I'm going to do. Want to race me up there?"

"I love you, Mom. But I don't want to run anywhere right now."

"Come with me in case I get lost."

"Sure." He gave her a quirky smile, then took her hand. "Come."

Reggie accompanied them from the room, and Grace stood to leave too.

Logan noticed and said, "Please don't go yet. I won't be long."

The pleading expression on his face made her heart race.

CHAPTER 8

Standing in front of the fire, Grace drew in several deep breaths. The pleasant, homey atmosphere in the cottage had soothed her spirit and reminded her of items on *her* bucket list. She didn't want to wait until outside influences prompted her to fulfill her desire to have a family. A loving family.

Logan reentered the living room and gathered cups and plates onto the tray. "Thanks for staying. I hope you didn't mind Mother's load of questions."

"Not at all. I enjoyed the evening and the convivial chatter. Is she all right?"

"Yeah. It's the sundowner effect. She often gets more confused later in the day. Tonight, the confusion came on suddenly."

"That must be hard on her. And you."

He nodded and sat on the sofa. "It is. That's why we are covering as much as we can from her bucket list."

"I think it's a wonderful act of love." She perched on the edge of the other sofa. Suddenly overcome by a desire to open up as she'd never done before, she said, "I wish I'd had a close bond with my, um, mother."

He frowned. "Tell me."

His soft words of encouragement were all she needed. "My adoptive parents weren't mean, but they were distant and cold. As I said, I joined the family when I was five. They had a daughter, Faye, then aged seven and they probably thought I would be good company for her. Faye and I liked each other, but I wasn't as quiet as she was, and always had questions. I think I got on Bernice's nerves, my mother. And then…" Grace hadn't shared details about her illness for many years and hesitated to open the old wound.

Logan quickly moved and sat beside her. "What happened?"

She released a big sigh. "Faye and I contracted meningitis. Bernice was suspicious of doctors and didn't take us until my sister was very ill. She died, and the high fever left me with severe hearing loss." A shoulder hike and another sigh. "And I thought life was hard before Faye's death. Of course, Bernice blamed me because I liked to play with the children down the street. Kids she considered poor white trash and assumed I contracted the illness from them."

"Meningitis is highly contagious."

"I know. Faye and I shared a bedroom. I carried around the guilt of causing her death for a long time. Until my teenage years when I remembered Faye got sick before me." She shoved those events back into the memory box where they belonged and gave Logan a small smile.

"How did *that* little girl become Dr. Grace Gentry?"

"I was smart and curious, and although I didn't get hearing aids until the school nurse intervened, I worked hard in school and was fortunate enough to later have a high school science teacher who insisted I apply for university scholarships." She nestled back into the cushions, comfortable in the cozy room with Logan "And that, as they say, is history."

"You overcame substantially high hurdles."

"I did." The warmth in the room or the reaction to his praise caused a flush she was sure he'd notice.

"Why did you accept the assignment at Oxford? Have you been a visiting professor before?"

"This is my first overseas teaching post." She pursed her lips against the rest of the answer, then added quickly, "I needed a change in scenery. Robbie, my late husband, and I worked in the same department at Tulane University in Louisiana. There were too many reminders of him there and in our home. I sold up and searched for other options where I could concentrate on the job."

"And here you are. I'm impressed you don't hold God responsible for your childhood woes and the accident."

Her eyebrows flew up. "What made you say that?"

"You went to church last Sunday."

She chuckled. "I'm not ashamed to admit I'm a follower of Jesus Christ. I try to live out my Christianity by the way I treat people. I attend services wherever I am."

"Which you wouldn't do if you were at odds with God."

A moment of inspiration hit her. "You mean like you are?"

He looked askance at her. "Whoa. No fair changing the focus to me."

"Perfectly fair. I've shared some pretty personal details with relative strangers tonight. Now it's your turn." She stared at him without blinking.

Myriad expressions touched his face, from anxiety to acquiescence, and then he crossed his legs, balancing one ankle on the other knee. "Fair is fair. I was raised in a Christian home. Attended Sunday school, summer church camp, et cetera, but I lost my way in university and—"

"Logan, Logan, where is Corey?" Irene called from the stairs. "You told me he'd be coming to see his Nana. You know he's my one-and-only."

Without hesitating, Logan left the room.

Grace was aware he spoke to his mother and guided her back up the stairs, but she couldn't make out much of the conversation.

When he returned, he stood by the fireplace and shook his head. "Sorry for the interruption. Mother is really agitated tonight."

"It's time for me to go." Although eager to hear about Corey, Grace stood and headed to the front door.

Logan followed. "Reggie is with Mother, and I *am* going to walk you home. No argument." He handed Grace her coat then slipped on his.

Once ambling side by side down the street, she shoved her hands into her pockets and asked, "Irene has a grandchild?"

"Yes. He's obviously on her mind." He hesitated then added, "And on mine. As I mentioned previously, I went off the rails in university and dated a girl I thought was "the one". We had, have a child. Corey is twelve years old. I was twenty-one when he was born, still working on my undergrad degree. Not enough sense to settle down." He glanced to the side. "He lives with his mother in Dallas. She's happily married, and I don't see Corey often. My fault."

He had a child, a son. "You must miss him."

"I do. When I resume my practice, I plan to see him frequently and become more involved in his life."

"Where will you work?"

"I have no idea. I, um, had a practice in Cypress, a community in northwest Houston, but I'm fighting a legal battle." He slowed his steps. "A co-worker falsely accused me of misdiagnosing a child who later passed away. Adrian Kerns, the co-worker, has since been arrested, but my reputation has suffered. Although I should be home rescuing my career, Mother's trip is more important right now."

Grace's opinion of him ratcheted up a notch. Putting his mother's needs above his own said a lot about his character. "My future residence and employment are also undecided. I don't know where I'll end up, either."

"It's most usual for me to share so much of my life with a person I only met four days ago."

Only four days? He knew more about her than her students did. "No problem. I'm glad you felt comfortable enough to do so."

"You're a good listener. I am too, in case you want to share more."

Grace giggled. "I'm also reticent about sharing. I keep my personal life in a box and only open it on rare occasions. Like now. With you."

They turned left on Sherborne Street and walked in

silence for a bit, then he placed his hand on her forearm.

"What's wrong?" she asked.

"Nothing, but I have a rather personal question. Was your adoptive family religious?"

She bit her bottom lip and shook her head, determined not to dwell on their definite lack of spiritual values.

"Then how did you come to know Christ?"

"The science teacher I told you about studied the Bible with me and invited me to the church he and his family attended."

"Interesting. Science and the Bible don't usually mix."

"I've heard that many times, but I disagree." On reaching her front door, she stopped and faced him. "I want to share my reasons with you, and I want to know why you lost your way, as you stated, but another day, okay?"

"Yes. I'll invite you to the cottage again."

"I'd like that. Thanks for the meal and the company. I hope you had a happy birthday. Um, given Corey's age, that makes you…thirty-four."

"I did. Especially celebrating with you."

Whew. He sure knew how to make her blush. "I have to go."

"One last question. Make that two. Is Brandeis the only place you applied to? And where in Texas did you apply?"

"Brandeis chose someone else."

"Are you disappointed?"

Used to fighting for every position she ever held, she shrugged. "I also interviewed with Rice University via Zoom and applied to the University of Texas in Austin. No interview yet."

"Houston or Austin? Interesting."

"Why?" Owls hooting in the nearby trees punctuated her question with their own.

"Mother lives in Round Rock, north of Austin, and a buddy from med school has a booming practice in the area. She's asked me to join her. However, it all depends on Mother's needs. When she can no longer live in her home, even with a full-time companion, I'll have to decide on a memory care facility for her. Of course, I want to be as close to her as possible."

He followed her through the gate to the front door.

"Wouldn't it be ironic if we both end up in Austin?" She opened the door and light from the hall illuminated him, all his six-foot height and broad shoulders hidden under his jacket.

He beamed at her. "That's not the word I'd used." He stepped to the walkway and then turned. "I'd say fortuitous, auspicious. Even propitious." He raised his hand in a wave and continued through the gate to the sidewalk.

As Grace giggled, he stopped and turned. "What now?"

"I had my thirty-sixth birthday in July. From now on you have to treat me as your superior."

He doffed an imaginary hat and grinned. "Yes, ma'am."

Grace closed the door and leaned against it. Again, deep breaths helped calm her racing heart. She climbed the stairs slowly, not wanting the contentment to end.

CHAPTER 9

Eager to see Grace, Logan hurried through breakfast, but his plans were put on hold when Mother asked him to take her to Broadway.

"Why do you want to go there again?" He managed to keep his tone congenial.

"I want to see the tower."

"We went there the day before yesterday."

"You're mistaken. We saw the tower from the parking area. I want to climb it today."

Logan glanced at Reggie seated beside Mother.

The woman shrugged. "She's been talking about it all morning."

Although they had entered the tower on the previous visit, Logan went along with his mother's request. "It's an uphill walk from the parking lot, Mother. Are you sure that's what you want to do?"

Irene thumped the table and silverware rattled on the plates. "Yes. I told your dad I'd meet him on the roof."

Wow. She hadn't mentioned his father in years.

Confusion so early in the day was a new symptom. How could Logan distract his mother without upsetting her? He tried changing the subject which had worked in the past. "Can I get you a special cup of coffee from the café you like by the river?"

Irene squinted and pursed her lips. "No. Let's get in the car before you forget how to drive."

So much for a distraction. Logan gathered their coats while Reggie carried the dishes to the sink.

"I'll stay here and clean up. You two have fun." She hugged Irene and then swiped at a tear trickling down her face. "See you later. Oh, don't forget to order the tickets before you go."

Logan hurried upstairs, opened his laptop, and bought the tickets online. Returning to the foyer, he shook his head. What Mother wanted at this stage, he was more than willing to provide. After settling her in the front seat, he reversed out of the garage and noticed a man standing against the wall on the other side of the street. Sure it was the same person he'd seen in the village center, he pointed. "Mother, see that man? Do you recognize him?"

She gave him a cursory look. "No. Let's go, please. I don't want to be late."

If she wasn't in such a hurry, Logan would have approached the guy. Next time.

The short trip only took twenty minutes. By now, Logan was used to the narrow, winding roads through quintessential English countryside. If he wasn't so preoccupied with seeing Grace again, he would have enjoyed another trip through the fall-colored scenery.

Mother said little, but as they parked, she fidgeted with the buttons on her coat, then removed a comb from her small purse and combed her hair over and over. Eventually, Logan removed the object from her. "You look beautiful, Mother."

A satisfied smile spread across her face. "I'm ready."

Logan followed her up the hill toward the tower. Halfway there, she took his arm and increased her stride. Nothing amiss with her stamina. When they reached the front doors, he expected her to swing them wide open and head to the stairs.

However, she turned and surveyed the area. "I need to sit down."

He'd noticed a bench on the other side of the tower when they visited the roof access previously and drew her in that direction.

She tugged on his coat sleeve. "Why are we here again?"

The morning's confused state had abated, and Logan wouldn't remind her of her request. "I thought you might like to see the tower one more time before we head to London." Alzheimer's or not, concocting a plan to meet his father here was bizarre, to say the least. Logan had only seen him twice since he walked out on the family twenty years ago and just the thought of meeting him soured his stomach.

They found the vacant bench bathed in weak sunshine and sat facing the Cotswold countryside. Mist played in the valleys and occasionally exposed orange and yellow foliage.

She took his hand in both of hers. "I know my memory is playing tricks on me so I want to discuss your future while I still remember who you are."

A lump the size of a grapefruit formed in Logan's

throat.

"That young lady who had supper with us last night—"

"Grace." He managed to sneak her name past the restriction.

"Yes. Grace. A lovely girl, uh, woman. Intelligent, sensitive, a survivor. I like her, and I know you do, too. I noticed how you look at her and I think you might be falling for her." Mother squeezed his hand then let go.

Logan stared at her. How did she discern so much in the short time Grace was at the cottage? But she was right. He did like Grace. A lot.

Arms folded, Mother looked into the distance. "I once read about the signs a person exhibits when she might be falling in love. This was long after the divorce and a doctor at the clinic and I had been dating for a while and he proposed—"

"Mother! How come I'm just now finding out about this? I knew you dated some, but marriage?"

"Quit interrupting me." She playfully slapped at his shoulder. "I wasn't about to share my love life with my teenage son."

No more than he'd have shared his with her. "So, what happened?"

"I reviewed the list of signs I'd found in a magazine and decided I wasn't in love. I was flattered by his attention, but I did not want another marriage. Been there. Done that. Now, son, listen to me."

She paused, so he replied, "Yes, Mother."

Slipping a piece of paper from her pocket, she cleared her throat. "I thought about you this morning and wrote down what I remembered, in no particular order. As I review the signs, I want you to look deep into your heart to see if they apply to you and Grace. Ready?"

He nodded.

"You think about her all the time."

"Check."

"You want to know how she feels about you."

He chuckled. "Definite check."

"You want to share your life with her."

He hadn't thought about spending a life together, but the prospect did sound wonderful. "Check."

"You want to keep her safe."

Grace reminded him of a perfect little doll. He'd have to be careful not to smother her. "Check."

"You want to make her happy."

"Naturally. Check."

"And this last one I added. You want to be a better person because of her."

That point hit him square between the eyes. He stood and took a few steps away from the bench and rubbed his chin. Since knowing Grace, he hadn't changed his behavior—no, he had. He didn't try to schmooze with her, he'd shown a genuine interest in her work, and he hadn't plied her with superficial flattering words. He wanted Grace to be proud of him and his actions. To be willing to introduce him to friends and colleagues and brag about his attitude or accomplishments. Yup. He'd have to make changes to his life. Even if Grace didn't return his feelings, he wanted to be that better person. A person who needed to reevaluate his relationship with God.

Logan sat beside his mother again and knowing how astute she was, asked, "Did you see anything in Grace's behavior that might indicate how she feels about me?"

His mother snuggled next to him. "I'm cold. And hungry. I want fish and chips for lunch. In…I don't care where."

No answer to his question. He tried again. "Let's return to the car and I'll find a good place for lunch. Um, Mother, do you think Grace likes me?"

Arm hooked through his, she walked carefully down the slope. A long minute later she said, "My head feels funny. Thoughts are jumping around as if they're on a trampoline. Let me try to sort them out." She hummed for a few seconds. "Okay. Yes, I think Grace likes you. Be careful, my boy. She's fragile and has been hurt."

"I know, Mother. She's special."

"Where's that car? I'm so cold."

Once in the vehicle, Logan turned on the heater and Googled a restaurant that served fish and chips. He found one in the village of Broadway, about five miles away.

As they drove along High Street—every village they'd visited seemed to have a High Street—his mother sucked in a breath and pointed to a church building on the right. "Oh, my lands. Stop the car, Logan."

A parking spot opened along the sidewalk. Before he'd turned off the ignition, she opened her door and ran toward the building. Logan followed and caught up with her as she reached the dark double doors.

"Let's see if we can go inside."

"Why, mother?"

"This is where I met your father."

"Wait. What? He was English?"

"No. He was visiting relatives in the area."

"And why were you here?"

"When I was eleven years old, I came to England with Grandfather Gee. Just the two of us. He had business to attend to in a café across the road. He left me to my own devices, and I wandered over here because I heard beautiful singing. It must have been a Sunday morning. George was roaming around the building, and we got to talking. We were the same age and hit it off. He was lonely and wanted to go back home to Texas. We decided to write to each other. But when I told Grandfather the boy's name and he was staying in…the name will come to me. Oh, yes. Rissing something. He got really angry and forbade me to write." She hurried back to the car.

Upper Rissington. Logan had seen the road sign. He ran after her. "Mother, did you write? Keep in contact?"

"No. I wouldn't disobey Grandfather Gee." She allowed Logan to open her door and slipped into the car.

Behind the wheel, he asked, "When did you meet again?"

A slow smile spread across her face. "Now, I said I didn't write to him, but I asked Regina to. You know, Reggie, my dear friend."

"You sly dog. And that's how you kept in touch."

"Yup."

Logan drove to the restaurant, waiting for Mother to provide more details, but she added nothing. He thought she'd lost her train of thought and decided he'd check with Reggie later.

However, once their meal had been served, Mother

munched on a piece of crispy fish, then said, "I never did find out what Grandfather had against George, but when I told him who I was marrying, he had a stroke and—"

"Are you serious?"

"Yes. He never regained consciousness and died two days before the wedding."

"Based on photos of him, I think he must have been a formidable figure. Why was he called Gee?"

"Let me think." Mother tapped a finger to her cheek. "His full name was George Elliot."

"Hmm. Maybe he wanted to be the only George in your life."

CHAPTER 10

By two o'clock, Mother had consumed all her fish and most of the chips along with downing three glasses of water, and now she was anxious to get home.

Early into this trip, Logan had resigned himself to spending the days doing whatever Mother asked. Today's adventure had revealed many interesting and even strange events, and he didn't regret the time he spent with her.

During the ride back to Burton, she frequently looked at him and smiled, but the blank expression on her face reminded him that their extensive conversations had probably sapped her emotional energy as well as depleted her memory vault.

Once home and settled on the sofa, Mother's mood darkened quickly. She mumbled and stared at her surroundings as if they were unfamiliar. Logan took her vitals. Blood pressure higher than usual, pulse rate more rapid than he liked, and slightly elevated temperature. Other than occasional sniffs, sneezing, and a niggling cough, she exhibited no major symptoms. All she wanted was a cup of tea and to go to sleep. Reggie helped settle her in bed and when she was asleep, returned to the living room with Logan.

He wanted to question her about writing to his father but decided to leave the matter for another day. He did, however, ask about Mother's medications.

"As you suggested, I keep her weekly med container in my room."

"Does she have access to any other medications?"

"No. At least, not that I know of. Do you want me to, um, search her room?"

"Please. Her behavior all day has been erratic. First, she's talking about my dad, then she's rational and discussing Grace." Logan frowned. "Almost as if she hadn't taken her prescription meds."

"I gave them to her this morning. That's not the issue. Maybe her disease is progressing faster than we expected."

He walked out to the small garden, pulled the last rose toward his nose, and sniffed the faint fragrance, Reggie's comment made sense, but he was loathe to accept the fact.

Although keen to visit Grace, his concern for his mother kept him home. After he and Reggie had a light evening email, he took Mother's temperature again. Same as before, however, she was restless and mumbled in her sleep.

He went to bed, but woke frequently and descended the stairs to listen at her ajar door. Although she coughed a time or two, he heard nothing else to alarm him. Back in bed but sleeping fitfully, creaking floorboards jarred him awake. Not the intermittent sounds of someone entering his room, but rhythmic creaks repeated over and over. He eased out of bed. Enough streetlight entered through the windows allowing him to explore without turning on the lamp. He ventured into the small alcove at the landing, remembering just in time to duck and avoid the low beams. Mother sat in the rocking chair, gently pushing herself back and forth as if on her porch at home. He'd never known her to sleepwalk, but approached her and gently touched her shoulder. "Mother."

She stirred, stopped rocking, and looked up at him. "I need tissues and I'm cold."

No wonder. She only wore her nightgown. "Let's get you back to bed."

As he helped her down the stairs to the second floor, he ran a hand across her forehead. Warm. Much warmer than it should be. Once she snuggled beneath the covers, he took her temperature. Almost one hundred one.

By now, Reggie entered the room. "Can I help?"

"Please. Get her a pitcher of water and a glass, and box of tissues."

He dampened a washcloth in the bathroom and bathed her face and neck and made her drink a little water. She blew her nose, then wadded a fresh tissue in her hand.

"Are you going to give her any medication?" Reggie asked.

"Not yet. I'll wait to see if the liquid intake and rest help. I have decongestion meds, but they might interfere with her blood pressure."

"I can stay with her."

"Thanks. I'll get the duvet from my room and sleep in here."

Seconds later, Reggie returned. "Here's the cover from the other bed in my room. Call if you need me."

"I will."

Throughout the night, Logan kept up the regime of bathing Mother's face and encouraging her to drink. She was restless but cooperated, and when he took her temperature, he was relieved to see it hadn't risen, and her pulse rate had slowed. He used his stethoscope and determined her lungs were clear. Good. Not pneumonia.

By dawn, her temperature was almost normal, but she was exhausted and wanted no food, only hot, sweet tea. Logan gave in and administered meds to ease her congestion and monitored her condition throughout the morning. At noon, he was heartened when she asked to bathe and go downstairs for a snack. While Reggie assisted her, he called Grace. He had to leave a voicemail message, and to hide his disappointment, he thumped the pillows and duvet he'd arranged for Mother on one of the sofas.

Chicken and lentil soup Reggie had made the previous day, along with buttered baps, satisfied Mother. She curled up under the covers and found a movie to watch on TV. Reggie sat on the other sofa, busy on her laptop. Logan closed the living room door to help keep the heat from the fireplace in the room.

With Mother on the mend, Logan walked to Grace's house and slid a note into the mail slot. He asked her to visit the cottage as he didn't want to leave the recovering patient for too long.

Mid-afternoon, the doorbell rang.

Logan opened the door and wanted to scoop up Grace in his arms. Instead, he said, "You read my note?" *Duh. Of course, she had.* "Thanks for coming.

Would you like some tea?"

"No, thanks. I'm sorry Irene is ill." Grace held out a small bouquet. "I can't stay long."

Before he could suggest she take the flowers to Mother, Reggie left the living room, closing the door behind her. "Irene is asleep. I'm going upstairs for a bit. Hello, Grace." She carried her laptop with her as she squeezed past them in the foyer.

"I'll give Mother the flowers as soon as she wakes. Very thoughtful of you." Logan took the bouquet and entered the kitchen.

"What's wrong with her?"

"At first, I dreaded she had pneumonia, but she responded to rest and plenty of liquids."

"There's a hospital in Moreton-in-Marsh."

"I know, thanks. When we arrived at the cottage, I did an online search. Mother didn't complain of having a headache or stiff neck. And not much of a cough. I'll keep a close watch and take her if her symptoms worsen."

"Sorry, of course, you're a doctor. Can I do anything?"

Not for Mother, but I'd like your company. "No, thanks. Reggie is a great help. Naturally, I have plenty of over-the-counter meds." He wanted to change Grace's mind and invite her for supper, but she received a text which she checked.

"Hmm. Marcus says someone came by the site asking what we'd found. It's not the same guy who messed with the bones earlier. I'd better go back."

Logan walked out with her, all the while quelling the desire to accompany her. But Bourton-on-the-Water was a small village, and he knew where to find her.

~~~

No amount of persuasion convinced Mother to stay home Sunday morning.

"I don't need any more rest, Logan, and as you said, my…setback…is not contagious." She paused, coffee mug in hand, and squinted at him. "Will you come with me, please?"

He hesitated as a barrage of excuses rammed his brain, many of them lame and all harked back to his teenage years when he'd been criticized by some people in Mother's church. But Logan had mellowed over the years and no longer considered the opinions of those church members relevant let alone his reason for not worshipping.

The real reason—dragged to the forefront of his mind when Grace asked him why he was at odds with God—he'd never revealed to Mother, and he wasn't about to now.

"No, Mom. I would just be occupying a pew." Nothing hypocritical with that statement.

She beckoned him closer and pretended to whisper, "Grace might be there."

He couldn't believe she'd tried to bribe him. "No matter. If I go it will be because I need to go, not because…"

"Sorry, son. That was unfair of me. I completely agree, and I'm sorry."

Bundled against the chilly wind, the ladies climbed out of the SUV at the church building. Logan parked in the side street and then walked down High Street in search of a good cup of coffee. He'd heard tales about the crowded conditions along the river during the summer, of people spreading blankets on the lawn and
~~~

camping out all day. He imagined the ducks fled for safety when the kids and dogs frolicked in the cool water.

He nodded to an elderly couple ambling together, each holding the leash of a non-descript dog that sniffed tufts of grass. The couple sat, their arms intertwined. Mother hadn't asked to sit by the river since being in Bourton. Odd. Logan would have thought the river held many memories for her. Pleasant ones, he hoped. Tomorrow, if she was feeling up to a stroll and the weather cooperated, he'd make the suggestion.

Coffee cup in hand, Logan returned to the riverbank, but as he walked, his heart seemed to grow heavier and heavier, weighed down by regret. Regret at not being man enough to own the real reason he stopped worshipping. He hadn't dwelt on that tumultuous time in his life for many years. He sat on a bench beneath the Bourton-on-the-Water sign and sipped his latte. When he discovered the youth minister at their church had been having sex with several girls in the group, and one of them was pregnant, Logan had run away. Literally. He was gone for three days, and when he returned home, he gave Mother a sob story about going to meet his dad who never showed.

He ditched his empty cup in the trash can and strode along the lawn beside the river. He kicked at bright, colorful leaves strewn about. Ducks quacked and swam lazily by, not scared off by a lone human.

That youth minister had apologized to the congregation and had been fired, but not before Logan avoided any dealings with the church or the people. Even Mother. When he went off to university, he seldom communicated with her, choices that added to his regrets.

Before he knew it, Logan had walked as far as he could beside the Windrush. Hands in his pockets he retraced his steps. He never stopped believing in the one true God, or the Bible as His word, but as far as going to church was concerned, he hadn't even thought about it until Grace summed up his situation in one sentence.

He sat on a different bench, elbows on his knees, his face cupped in his hands. At first, he'd blamed Tyler, the minister, for having a child outside the bonds of marriage. *If he can, so can I.* But long ago, Logan had accepted responsibility for his actions. While twirling a leaf stem between his fingers, a stabbing pain in his chest made him straighten. What? Not a heart attack, but an attack of conscience. The reason for the trip with Mother, his uncertain career future, and his brief association with Grace had all combined to make him reevaluate his priorities.

Marching to his car, he smiled. After lunch, he would visit Grace and tell her why he *had been* at odds with God. Past tense.

Reggie and Mother especially enjoyed the Sunday roast lunch at the corner pub. Nothing wrong with her appetite today. When the ladies were settled back at the cottage, Logan made sure the fire blazed in the living room and the thermostat for the rest of the downstairs area was also set to keep them warm, then he set off for the dig site.

His brisk walk was rewarded by seeing the van in the lot and activity under the canopies.

"Hey, Marcus." He looked around. One student worked with Marcus and two were at the other site.

"Y'all look busy."

"We are."

"Do hikers ever stop by and ask what's going on?"

"Not often. Oh, a few days ago, a guy did stop and ask a load of questions. I didn't like the look of him, but it wasn't the same man who hit me. This chap was tall, older, and didn't cover his face."

"Grace told me when you texted her. Has he been back?"

Marcus shook his head, making his curls flop over his forehead. "I'm glad she decided to keep the bones secure in the van."

"Is she in the tent?"

"No. She was called back to Oxford. I drove her to the station in Moreton-in-Marsh this morning."

Shoulders sagging, he asked, "When will she be back?"

Marcus shrugged and returned to brushing dirt off an object in the hole.

The trip back to the cottage took way longer. Logan trudged down the road as if physically carrying his heavy heart.

CHAPTER 11

As spruced up as she could be, Grace sat in front of the computer in Peggy's office and took a sip of water. She'd conducted two Zoom interviews already and should be comfortable with the process by now, but she had to fight the desire to hide under the desk. The interview with the Archeology Department at the University of Texas in Austin couldn't be any harder. Tempted to brush her hair behind her ears, she stopped in time when she remembered how they protruded. *Leave it be. They won't be interested in your physical attributes.*

Notebook to her left, Grace repeated the words she'd written in large letters across the first page. "You are qualified. You've led five excavations in three countries. You correctly identified the causes of death at a mass burial site when other experts suggested the deaths weren't linked. You can do this."

She glanced at her muted cell phone and recalled the conversation she'd had with Logan the previous evening. When she told him the reason for her sudden trip to Oxford, he encouraged her to be herself, but to be direct and forceful in her answers, and to pretend he was one of the interviewing panel. "Provide information even an observer like me can understand."

The screen icon appeared, and Grace clicked on the "join meeting" box. She introduced herself, then as the members made introductions, decided which one would be Logan. The panel of five consisted of three men and two women. That in itself, pleased Grace. The other interviews were conducted by men only. She decided the man in the middle would be Logan. He had similar grayish-blond hair and a ready smile. During the interview, she didn't have to rely on her notes once and remembered to look into the camera instead of at the pictures of the people on the screen.

"We have two other candidates to interview. We'll get back to you by the end of the week."

And with that concluding statement, the interview ended. Grace sagged into the chair. She never speculated on the results of an interview. The panel had two more candidates lined up—this was going to be a long week. She checked the wall clock in Peggy's office. Just after five. No wonder her shoulders ached from the tense position she held in front of the computer. The time difference between England and Austin necessitated scheduling the interview in mid-afternoon which had given Grace the morning to discuss many things with her boss. Foremost was the future of the excavation in Bourton. Peggy wanted Grace and her crew to continue at the third dig, stating the hands-on experience at the unusual site could only benefit the students.

Grace gathered her belongings into her small

overnight bag and headed down the corridor in search of Peggy. After quizzing Grace on the interview, she suggested a meal out before taking her to the station.

Seated at the table, Peggy stabbed a fork into her seafood salad. "How is my brother?"

"Sir Barrette has only come to the site once, but he does email me for updates."

"Good. Since the dig has provided useful exposure to the students, I'm glad he asked for my help."

"I am, too." Grace sipped her lemonade. "Bourton-on-the-Water is such a lovely village."

"The town center is on a river, right?"

Grace nodded and swallowed the last bite of salmon. "The Windrush flows right through it."

"With several stone bridges."

"That's correct. By the way, thank you for letting me use the department's Zoom account for these interviews."

"You are welcome. We want our favorite visiting professor to find a wonderful new position."

Once seated on the train, Grace called Marcus. She hadn't given him the reason she had returned to Oxford but filled him in now.

"How did the interview go?"

"As usual, I'm not sure. But I hope I'm offered the position which is at the Texas Archeology Research Lab, with some time allocated to working with students. But the best part is the university will allow me, if hired, to work with local authorities when a forensic anthologist is needed."

"Right up your alley."

"Yep."

"I have to tell you what happened yesterday. I—"

She straightened. "Not more trouble over the bones?"

"Well, not trouble. We found three sets of skeletal remains in Tertius. So far, only a couple of bones from each body. Two children and an adult."

"You're taking photos and documenting finds in the log?"

"Definitely. You taught us well, Dr. Gentry. We're placing the bones in storage tubs right away so we can keep them in the van overnight."

Although she wasn't present at the initial find, the usual surge of adrenaline warmed her blood. "I can't wait to see the site. Please, pick me up in fifteen minutes."

"I'll set out right now, but there's more."

"More bones?"

"No, no. I have to tell you about Logan."

"What about him?" Surely, he and Irene hadn't left the village? Her pulse quickened.

"He came to the site yesterday, late afternoon. When I told him you'd gone to Oxford, his reaction was priceless. I've never seen a facial expression change so quickly. He was disappointed, to say the least."

Another bit of news to warm her. "Thanks for telling me."

"Have you spoken to him?"

"Yes. I called him last night and told him why I went to Oxford. He…" She wasn't sure how much to tell Marcus. Her private life was none of his business. She needn't have worried.

"I'd say that guy has it bad."

"It?"

"Oh, come on, Dr. Gentry. You must have guessed

his interest in our site has nothing to do with the Romans." He chuckled. "See ya in a few minutes."

Smiling, she leaned back and closed her eyes. She'd prayed over each interview, but it seemed she'd made an extra plea for the job in Austin. The fact Logan might end up living there hadn't entered her mind.

CHAPTER 12

The suggestion to walk along the Windrush had filled Mother with awe. She said she'd forgotten a river meandered through the village. Which was strange as she and Reggie had to cross the river when they visited the Model Village. However, drizzle fell throughout Monday and Logan had to postpone their plans. With Grace in Oxford, he'd spent the day playing board games with Mother and Reggie and communicating with his lawyer in Texas.

When the sun dawned in a cloudless sky on Tuesday, he gave Mother a thumbs-up. She hurried through breakfast, refused a second cup of tea, and had her coat and scarf ready before Logan had even shaved.

"We need to wait an hour or two, Mother. Let the sun take the chill out of the air."

"Oh, all right. I'll crochet until then. I've almost finished the blanket so it should be ready for Marge's granddaughter who is due next month."

Reggie presented Mother with her morning meds which she swallowed with sips of water.

"Thanks, Reg. I, we, really appreciate your help. I hope you're enjoying the trip."

"Yes, indeed. Thank you for paying my way. This is my first time in the UK. I especially liked Edinburgh."

Logan returned upstairs as Mother and Reggie discussed the military tattoo they'd attended. No confusion this morning, which boded well for a good day. He shaved quickly, eager to take Mother to the river and listen to her good memories associated with it.

By ten o'clock, the temperature had risen enough for their jaunt. Reggie opted not to join them, stating she needed to purchase a few ingredients to make the chili Mother had requested.

Arm in arm, Logan and his mother walked down Victoria Street and crossed the river to the north side where the dappled sunshine played among the leaves on the grass. She made a few comments about the buildings she recognized, but mostly it seemed, she was absorbing the ambiance. He purchased two cups of hot cocoa, then directed her to a bench about halfway down the High Street.

"Are you warm enough?"

"Yes, son. The hot drink helps."

"What do you remember about the river?"

She sipped the cocoa. "Playing in the water. It's not deep, you know."

"I know."

"I notice lots of changes, but it's still so peaceful and beautiful."

"I agree. I'm glad Bourton was on your bucket list."

"Why?"

"Because this is where the Windrush flows." He smiled and glanced at the pedestrian bridge where he'd first encountered Grace. "I met Grace…" he pointed, "on that bridge over there." *And I saved her from a dunking in the water.*

"It's a pretty river, and I like the name. Windrush makes me think of something romantic. Magical even."

"Believe me, Mother, I agree." He frowned. Did she remember the discussion about Grace they had at the Broadway Tower? Before he could ask, a man approached the bench and slowed until he stood in front of them.

"Sorry to bother you. Are you Irene Quinn, nee Anderson?"

Logan glared at the man wearing a familiar green coat. His expression was sincere, so Logan didn't think he meant any harm, but he stood anyway and said, "Yes, this is Irene. Who are you?"

"Maybe we can talk somewhere private."

Logan glanced around. "I don't see anyone close by."

"Okay. My name is Nigel Stewart. My grandmother recently passed away and left me a journal to read after her death."

"Get to the point. I'm cold," Mother said.

"Do you want to go back to the cottage, Mother?"

"Please."

No one spoke on the short walk back to Cloisters. Logan opened the front door and was immediately surrounded by the savory aromas of sautéed onions and chili spices. He had no problem with Reggie hearing their discussion so he directed Nigel and Mother into the living room.

"What is your business with my mother, Nigel?" Logan sat beside her and took her hand.

"Not just with her, but with your whole family."

Reggie poked her head around the door. "Anyone for tea?"

"No, thanks. We had cocoa by the river." Until he discovered what Nigel wanted, Logan wasn't about to offer him any hospitality.

"There's no other way but for me to be direct. My grandmother indicated my grandfather, whom I never met, was an American stationed at the RAF base in Little Rissington during World War Two."

"Who was your grandfather?" Mother asked, her fingers tightened their grip on Logan's hand.

"George Elliot Anderson."

Mother gasped. "No. Not possible."

"Let's hear him out. What other evidence do you have?"

"My grandmother included my father's birth certificate which names George as his father." Nigel looked at Mother. "Your grandfather was stationed here during the war, wasn't he?"

She nodded.

"It all sounds…feasible." Logan shrugged. "You've been following me for a few days, but how did you know we'd be here?"

"I waited to approach you both in a public place." Nigel fluffed a cushion on the sofa. "That way, you couldn't slam the door in my face. I searched online and located George and your parents, Irene. All deceased. But I also found a Kenneth Anderson—"

"My brother. We, uh, haven't spoken in years."

"I took a chance and contacted him. He suggested

you had a closer relationship with Grandfather and might have known about his affair in England."

"I most certainly did not. Trust Kenny to get me involved."

"He told me you were on holiday and would be staying in Bourton."

Logan didn't have a high opinion of his uncle and this latest dig at Mother annoyed him. "How on earth would he know that?"

A clattering and a mumbled cuss word emanated from the kitchen. Logan rose and peeked into the room. "Everything okay, Reggie?"

"Yes. I dropped a saucepan lid."

He turned back to Nigel. "Well, it seems as if you and Mother are…cousins. What do you hope to glean from this relationship?" His great-grandparents hadn't been wealthy, and even if Nigel pursued legal action, there wouldn't be any financial compensation. Mother and Kenny had inherited their maternal grandparents' estate, but that wouldn't benefit any newfound kin.

"Just knowing who my grandfather was is enough. I'd always been told he died in the war, but to meet relatives who knew him was all I ever wanted. And maybe get a photo of him."

"I don't have any with me, but I can send one, a few when I get home." She nabbed a tissue and wiped her nose. "I'm tired, Logan."

"Other than that, are you feeling all right?" He placed his hand on her forehead. No fever.

"I'm fine, but I want to go upstairs. Meeting Nigel has been a shock. Get his address for the pictures."

Logan helped Mother off the sofa and as they walked through the kitchen, he asked Reggie, "Please take her up. I have more questions for our guest."

"Come along, Irene, dear."

On returning to the living room, Logan paced to the far corner and back. "A shock, for sure. How did your grandmother meet George?"

"Her name was Doris Stewart. She worked on base and, at that time, lived in Nether Westcote, a little village not far away. Their affair lasted several months."

"Did Doris know he was already married?"

"I don't think so. She doesn't address that topic in her journal."

Logan perched on the edge of the sofa opposite Nigel. "Did George know she had a child?"

"She didn't say. In her last letter to him, she told him she was pregnant, and that if it was a boy, she'd name him George. All letters she wrote after that were returned." Nigel hung his head. "She assumed he'd been killed."

Staring out the conservatory windows to the garden, Logan focused on the pink and lavender sweet peas still climbing the tall rose bush. The startling info about his great-grandfather didn't bother him, but it affected Mother. She'd idolized the man. Logan recalled the story she told of Grandfather Gee being so adamant she did not correspond with the boy named George she'd met. If he'd thought the kid was his grandson, named after another George, his action made sense. And later, her telling him the name of her groom might have triggered his stroke.

"I have a few more questions, Nigel. Did your grandmother have a boy and name him George?"

"She did and named him George Henry. At that

time, many young English girls married servicemen, local or American, and frequently ended up pregnant. My mother moved back home to Stow-on-the-Wold and told everyone her husband was dead. She opted to call her son Henry, I guess to ease the hurt of not seeing George again."

"I can understand that. Where do you live?"

"In Stow. I own the Wayfarer's Inn, and my son-in-law helps me run the place."

"Leave your address with me. After Mother has had a chance to digest this information, maybe we can visit before we head to London."

"I'd like that." Nigel placed a business card on the coffee table. "I'll see myself out. Goodbye."

Logan let out a hefty breath. Mother and Nigel were cousins, so his daughter was Logan's first cousin once removed? Second cousin? He never could keep the relationship words straight. The trip to England sure had its surprises. Which reminded him… He called Grace and had to leave a message.

Hearing rumblings upstairs, he checked in on Mother. "Anything wrong?"

"No. Reggie and I were just discussing my medications."

Logan raised an eyebrow toward Reggie.

"Irene likes to know what each pill is for. I was…describing their benefits. That's all."

Satisfied, he ran downstairs and sat out in the garden to check his email. More messages from Wayne Hammond, his lawyer. Although Logan's co-worker had been convicted of the child's death, he was filing appeals, which meant Logan would be involved. The sunshine and cooing pigeons weren't enough to brighten his mood, but when Grace returned his call, his heart would have somersaulted if not attached.

"Sorry, I missed your call. Is Irene all right?"

Just like her to be concerned about his mother. "Yes. Physically, but we had an unexpected visitor. I'll tell you about him later. I don't want to leave her while she's in an emotionally fragile state, so can you come for supper this evening? You can tell me all about your interview."

"I'd love to. See you at six?"

"Yes." Grinning like a kid in his own candy store, Logan entered the kitchen and opened the pot containing the chili. There might be enough for four people, but if not, he didn't care if he ever ate again. He'd see Grace, and that was all he needed.

CHAPTER 13

The skeletal remains found in Tertius kept Grace and her crew busy. She'd invited each member in turn to help her in the tent identifying and tagging the bones. At first, she'd agreed with Marcus that there were two children and one adult, but after a more detailed examination of additional bones found, she determined the third skeleton to be that of a teenager.

Taking advantage of another teachable moment, she called the team together after their lunch break. "What characteristics do we usually use to identify age at death?"

"It's easier if we have a complete skeleton, but the length of the long bones is a good indicator." Marcus pointed to the open tub holding the few bones of the children they'd found.

"Right. And for children, examining the mandibles is crucial."

"Which we don't have." Trust Susan to state the obvious.

Grace had laid out the bones for the older person

on the table. "Let's look at our third body. What characteristics will help identify his approximate age? I've asked Marcus not to share what he discovered to make him change his mind that this was an adult."

"Growth plates on the long bones disappear between seventeen and…twenty-five." Looming over the table, Charles picked up a femur. "Look here at the head. The greater trochanter has united with the bone, but the line of union is still visible. So, I'd say, he was in his early twenties."

"Good deduction. What else?"

"We do have some of his vertebrae. His sacrum has not completely fused. Again, this usually occurs during the same period at the growth plates fusing. And—"

"Wait, Kristie, don't monopolize the show. Let me add another characteristic. If we had his mandibles, we could examine his tooth eruption. An adult would have all his molars visible." Susan seemed obsessed with the mandibles.

"Correct, both of you. Marcus, tell us which one convinced you."

"At first, we only had part of his skull—the frontal bone with a prominent brow ridge. From that, I determined he could be male. We had one humerus, but the head was smashed. Later, we found his femurs and some vertebrae, including the sacrum. I based my assessment that he was in his late teens on those two characteristics."

"A tall teenager for sure. Good work, everyone." Grace slipped her hands into her pockets. "While I was in Oxford, I had an interview with the University of Texas. They will make a decision next week. Dr.

Wilson wants us to continue at this site, not necessarily to add to the extensive body of work already done here, but to provide you with more experience. Your book knowledge has been put to the test, and I'm proud of your deductions concerning the skeletal remains." She jutted her chin toward Kristy. "Do you think you and Charles have discovered all your site has to offer?"

"We haven't found any human remains for a while. The deeper we go, the more animal bones we find."

"Okay, team, I think we can close Secundus and all focus on Tertius, but I have one more question. A few days ago, Charles unearthed two charred adult bones in Secundus. A femur and a tibia. Keeping in mind we don't have a complete skeleton, any ideas as to why just these bones show evidence of being in a fire?"

"Maybe he was supposed to be cremated, and the ceremony was interrupted," Susan said.

"Or, those two bones belong to another male." Charles hiked a shoulder. "Since we don't have a pelvis, we can't be sure the femur is his."

Thumping his shoulder, Kristy said, "I agree with you."

Marcus frowned and looked at Grace. "What's your opinion, professor?"

She nodded. "I also agree with Charles. As we find remains, we need to remember the history of our location. We can't assume all the bones we find in an area belong to one human, especially if significant bones are missing. I think the charring occurred long after death." She held open the tent flap. "Back to work, everyone. Kristy, when you and Charles have filled in the Secundus site, you can assist Susan and Marcus."

The crew left the tent, and Grace returned the

teenager's bones to the tub. She set out the children's bones on the table. Young, judging by the length of the femurs. Five to seven years of age. No evidence of the cause of death yet. With four people excavating, they should locate more bones to help complete the skeletons.

Clouds blocked the sun all afternoon and dusk fell early. With all the bones secure in tubs in the van, Marcus drove the team back to their house.

Although Grace had not physically participated in the dig, she always marveled at how dirt seemed to creep under her clothes. Showered and changed into jeans and a pink sweater, she hurried downstairs and found Kristy in the living room. "I'm going out for supper. See you later."

"I bet I can guess who the lucky chap is."

"Who?"

"Logan, of course."

Warm from her shower and the flush flooding her face, Grace grabbed her coat and ran to Cloisters. She had not done a good job of hiding her feelings for Logan, and as she approached the cottage, she slowed and squared her shoulders. *I like him and I'm sure he likes me. So what are you going to do about it, Gracie, girl?*

Irene asked Grace to sit beside her again, but this time, she didn't swamp her with questions. After the best chili she'd had in a long time, Grace helped Logan carry dishes to the kitchen and rinsed them off while he stacked the dishwasher.

"No chocolate cake this evening." Reggie switched on the electric kettle. "Will you stay for tea, Grace?"

"Yes, thank you." Drying her hands, she stepped

away from the sink. "I could have brought a treat for dessert. Next time, I…" Her words hung in the air. Very presumptions of her.

"We do have a selection of cookies. Mother loves Custard Creams and Caramel Digestives, among others." Logan set a plate on the counter.

Reggie added the cookies and shooed Grace and Logan away. "Run along, you two. I'll bring in the tray."

Irene noshed on the cookies as if she hadn't just eaten a big meal. She and Reggie shared a sofa, and Grace and Logan occupied the other one.

The soft conversation and the pleasant room lulled Grace into a dream-like state where she imagined the "what-ifs". She vaguely heard Irene and Reggie banter back and forth and would have been content to stay in that frame of mind, but Logan suddenly leaned forward.

"Mother, are you all right?"

"Why does everyone keep asking me that? Of course, I'm fine. I must get ready for my meeting. Regina says I don't have a meeting, but I do." She stood and grabbed a magazine from the coffee table and fanned her face. "I'm hot."

Without a contradictory word, Reggie guided Irene from the room and up the stairs.

"Sorry for deserting you, Grace. I'll go up until Mother is settled. Please don't leave just yet."

Grace waited by the fireplace. Irene might deem the room too warm, but she thought the temperature was perfect.

Upon reentering the living room, Logan joined her at the fireplace. "Mother's behavior is so unpredictable. Nothing in my research into Alzheimer's prepared me for the reality of the disease's progression. Some days she's lucid and almost her old self, and other times she goes off the rails at a moment's notice."

Grace took his hand and guided him to the sofa. "If it's hard on you, imagine what she must be going through?"

"I know. I know." He hung his head. "I think we might have to draw our UK trip to a close sooner than planned. When she's back in her own home, among familiar things, the rapid changes might decrease."

"Oh, my dear Logan. I'm so sorry for her and you. This must be very painful." She rubbed his back and he straightened.

"Thank you for caring." He ran his fingers through his hair. "Okay, let's focus on something more positive. Tell me all about your interview."

She bent her knees, drew her legs up underneath her, and turned to face him. Recalling the process at first sent anxious knots to her stomach, but the more she talked to her rapt audience, the more confident she became that she'd aced the interview. "They're supposed to let me know by the end of the week. I've heard that before, but this time—"

"What if both Rice and UT offer you a job?"

"I don't think Rice will come through. One man on the panel, a senior member, sent out negative vibes." She rested against the cushions. "Oh, well. I know I gave both interviews my best and prayed for the right job."

He patted her knee. "Let me know as soon as you hear."

"I will. Now, tell me about the surprise visitor you had."

"Ooh. Seems my great-grandfather Gee had an affair while stationed here during World War Two. They had a son, although supposedly he didn't know about him, and that son had a son who visited us. Nigel lives in Stow-on-the-Wold."

Grace frowned. "Making him…Irene's cousin?"

"Right."

"How does she feel about having relatives in England?"

"Not too happy. Her opinion of her grandfather has been tarnished." Logan rubbed his temples. "The revelation might be contributing to her decline."

The next topic Grace wanted to discuss was harder to introduce. How could she determine if he'd decided where to set up his practice without coming right out and asking him? Although she'd discounted receiving an offer from Rice, what if she was offered both jobs? Before deciding, she'd love to know where he'd settle down. But he had a more pressing situation on his hands, and she refrained from asking.

However, he introduced a related subject himself. "I mentioned we might cut our trip short, but even if we don't, we'll head to London this Friday."

She recalled he'd told her when they'd be leaving the village, but his words acted like an ice-cold knife slicing into her heart. "So soon." *Had she uttered the phrase out loud?* "And you don't know how long you'll be there."

"No. Even if Mother's condition remains stable, I think it's time to take her back home." He looked at Grace as if he wanted to say more, but then he shook his head. "What's happening at the dig site? I want to visit again, if I may."

"Of course. Come anytime. We found bones from two children and a teenager in Tertius. The total number of humans we've uncovered is surprising. Even Dr. Wilson remarked on our finds."

"Depending on Mother, I might come tomorrow."

"When you return to Texas, will you live with Irene in Round Rock?" The question flew out of her mouth unbidden, but she didn't regret asking.

"Yes. Until my legal issues are resolved I can't take Dana Booth, my friend from med school, up on her offer to join her practice. Adrian Kerns is appealing his sentence, so the case might drag on and on."

"That's a shame. As if you don't have enough on your plate right now."

"I want—"

"Logan, can you come upstairs, please?" Reggie's voice held a note of panic. "Irene's trying to climb out the window."

"Be right there." He leaned toward Grace and cupped her face in his warm hands. "Sorry, I can't walk you home tonight." He kissed her on the cheek then stood and hurried out of the room.

As Grace walked home, a cold wind danced around her, tempting her to be disappointed, but she paid it no heed. All she could feel were Logan's thumbs tenderly caressing her cheeks as if they were covered in gold dust.

CHAPTER 14

Bright blue skies, good coffee, and Mother chatting up a storm all put Logan in a good mood. Aware they would be leaving Bourton in a couple of days, she wanted to walk around the village and have Reggie help her take photographs using her iPad. He reminded Mother he had hundreds of pictures, but she insisted she wanted to decide what to photograph.

"Is Birdland Park and Gardens too far to walk?" Reggie gave Mother her coat. "Irene has mentioned it a few times."

"I don't think so. Just in case you need it, here's a map of the village." He handed her the map he'd purchased at the Information Office and then kissed Mother on the forehead. "Enjoy your day. I'm going to see Grace. Can I invite her for supper again tonight?"

"Of course, son. I like her."

Logan jogged to the dig site and slowed as he neared the tent. A lilting melody plucked a memory chord in his brain.

"I sing because I'm happy. I sing because I'm free.

His eye is on the sparrow and I know he watches me."

He recognized Grace's sweet voice and slowly lifted the tent flap, hoping to hear more of the song and watch as she sang.

But she noticed him right away. "Oops. You caught me."

"I'll gladly wait outside if you'll sing again."

Pink infused her cheeks. "Sorry. No can do. Rather, no, won't do." She frowned. "You know what I mean."

"That's a beautiful song."

"It's an old hymn made popular by gospel singers."

He stepped closer to the table where she worked. "Do you just like the words, or do they have special significance? As in, happy because…"

"Happy because…oh, no. I haven't heard from Rice or UT. The song's been on my mind since my Bible reading this morning."

"Which was?"

"Matthew 6:26. 'Look at the birds of the air; they do not sow or reap or store away in barns, and yet your heavenly Father feeds them. Are you not much more valuable than they?' I constantly have to remind myself I'm valuable, and worthy to God because of His son's sacrifice for me. For the world."

Logan hung his head. If she needed reminders, how much more did he? "Um, I'll have to ask Mother if I can borrow her Bible and read that chapter." He stared at his shoes. Yeah, he'd really said those words.

Grace turned to him and gazed at his face, then smiled. "Do I detect a mellowing in your attitude?"

"Maybe." He cleared his throat. "Are those the

children's bones?" Duh. She certainly wasn't examining an adult's remains.

"Yeah. Two young kids. We haven't found enough yet to tell if they're male or female."

As Logan examined the small bones, he had a hard time differentiating between the two. "How can you tell which bones go together? I mean, to me, they all look to be the same age."

Grace picked up two femurs. "Nothing scientific, but plain common sense. I measure like bones against each other and set the longer of the pair in one area and the shorter one in another. Of course, that only works with the long bones. If there's only one bone, then I compare it to the others. Naturally, my method is flawed, but for our purpose here, it will work. Our excavation is not an active burial site where the forensic evidence would be used to determine who the children are, were."

"Is that your area of expertise?"

"Yes. One of the negative aspects of our site here is its history. We knew before coming that the chance of finding intact skeletal remains was next to zero. But I have enjoyed the excursion, and believe it or not, I've learned alongside my students. Take the young male we also found in Tertius."

Logan was learning, too, but he loved the passion in Grace's voice as she described what she was doing. She kept on explaining and pointing to different bones, and when he didn't respond, her voice trailed off.

"Dr. Quinn, are you paying attention?"

Jolted from his daydream, he stammered, "Yes, professor. Of course, professor."

They both burst out laughing as Marcus came

barging into the tent. "Hope I'm not interrupting?"

"Um, no. What's up?" she asked, chin high as if trying to increase her height.

"You're not going to believe what we found."

"Let's go see." She motioned Logan to follow her.

Marcus led the way to Tertius where Charles and Kristy squatted in the hole and beamed. Susan, standing on the rim of the dig, pointed to the freshest area excavated.

"I see you're increasing the size of the original dig. Moving further east into the slight rise."

"Yeah. The children's bones are scattered the other way, mostly broken ribs, vertebrae, carpals, and tarsals." Susan held several tiny bones in her gloved hand.

"Nothing unusual yet. What else?" Grace shielded her eyes against the sunlight.

Charles held his long arms out wide. "Ta-dah. A wall or other structure."

Bending, Logan looked beyond the two crew members in the hole. Side-by-side rectangular stones protruded from the gravel.

Grace accepted his helping hand to enter the dig. "So unexpected. It seems to extend into the mound. Marcus, give me the camera, please. I need closeup photos to examine."

"Do you want to join us?" Kristy asked.

"No. The site is already crowded. You arc all doing a great job. Follow the length of the wall and also see how far down it extends. Of course, finding bones is still our main focus." She accepted the camera and took several shots before handing it to Logan.

He helped her out and they headed back to the tent.

"What's the significance of the wall?"

"It all depends on the age of the structure. The mound where Tertius is located may not have been part of the gravel extractions. That means the wall wouldn't have been destroyed by the process." Grace transferred the pictures from the camera to her laptop.

Logan looked over her shoulder as she enlarged first one shot then another. She paid close attention to the mortar.

Chuckling, she shook her head. "The wall is very new, as in last century. Sir Barrette has three sons. I bet as young kids, they came down here and built themselves a fort or something. The mortar is a definitive giveaway." She picked up the camera. "I'll return this to Marcus and give the crew the news, disappointing as it may be."

Logan accompanied her, and on the way back to the tent, asked if she'd like to visit the cottage for a meal that evening. "I don't know what Mother and Reggie will be cooking, but I know there'll be plenty."

Inside the tent, she placed her hand on his arm. "Oh, I'd love to. But I have a conference call with my boss and other members of the department at seven. Can I take a rain check?"

"Of course."

"I'll bring dessert next time."

"Perfect. I'll—" His phone chirped, and he checked the screen. "A text from Reggie. They went walking this morning and are home. Mother wants me back for lunch." He backed up to the flap. "Bye. See you soon."

She tilted her head. "Don't forget what you said."

"I said a lot of things."

"About reading Matthew. In the Bible."

"Oh, yes. I will, just for you."

"No. Do it for you." Her smile took the edge off her words.

He jogged back to the cottage in a somber mood.

~~~

A gentle rain fell all the next morning and the forecast predicted a wet afternoon, too. Mother and Reggie worked in the living room, one crocheting and the other composing her life story, while Logan prepared lunch. He was making his famous—at least in Mother's eyes—mac and cheese. The local grocery store had a wonderful array of cheeses, some Logan hadn't tried before. Together with the ingredients he needed, he'd also purchased what Reggie required for her cottage pie. After lunch, Logan planned to visit Grace at the house, sure the crew was homebound and not at the dig site.

Logan served the meal on trays and joined the ladies in the living room. The flickering flames lifted the gloom the gray skies had heaped upon him. However, he was man enough to admit reading the passage in the Bible mentioned by Grace had not lifted his spirits at all. In fact, the event had sent him on a downward spiral of guilt and regret. He had to talk to her as she was the only person he could think of who'd rescue him.

After he cleaned up the kitchen, he hurried to the house.

She opened the door right after he knocked, almost as if she'd been waiting for his visit. "Come in."

"Thanks. I won't say long." He followed her to the living room where Marcus and Charles sat around the
~~~

fireplace. Not wanting to forecast his reason for coming, he greeted the men but didn't sit.

Grace seemed to understand. "Let's go to the dining room." She closed the door behind him and sat at the table.

He chose the chair beside her. "This is better. How are you? Any news?"

"Yep. Just received word from Rice. They offered the job to someone else."

"Oh, I'm sorry." Logan placed his hand on her forearm. "No, I'm not. Because I want you to get the UT job."

"Me too. I'm praying for that eventuality."

Her reply helped lift his spirits a tad. "What is everyone doing since you can't go to the dig?"

"Working on reports and I hope the crew is reading the latest assignments I've given them. And you?"

"Mother has almost finished the blanket for Marge's granddaughter. She was a bridesmaid for Mother, and they've remained good friends. She wanted to come with us, but her first grandbaby is due this month. Reggie is working on her biography." He leaned back and clasped his hands, twiddling his thumbs. "And I've been corresponding with my lawyer, playing solitaire, watching TV. Really important tasks."

"But you're close by if Irene needs you."

A knock on the door and Susan opened it and poked her head around. "Hey, Grace, I have a problem with the last reading you assigned."

"I'll be right with you."

Logan stood and waited for Susan to close the door then asked, "Can you join us for supper this evening?"

"I'd love to, and remember, I'll bring the dessert."

She walked him to the front door and opened it. "See you later."

Standing on the top step, he leaned close and whispered, "I, um, have something important to discuss with you."

She blushed but closed the door before he could clarify his statement. As he stood under the roof of the small porch, he frowned. He meant discussing the Bible reading with her, but if she interpreted the words to indicate he'd declare his feelings for her, well, why not? They were leaving Bourton the next day, and he did want Grace to know he was crazy about her. Wanted to keep in touch and continue the relationship when back in Texas, if she agreed. Expert anthropologist she might be, but she couldn't uncover what was in his heart unless he told her.

Disposition considerably lightened, he raised the hood of his jacket, and hands in his pockets, hurried home. He chuckled to himself. Why do most people run in the rain? They're probably already wet and running a few steps won't alter the fact. He walked the last block and entered the cottage where he removed his jacket and hung it up in the small bathroom.

Mother helped Reggie with the menu, peeling potatoes and carrots. Logan set the table in the conservatory and made sure the heating was turned on.

Grace arrived at six and handed him a box filled with delicacies from a bakery in the village. "I didn't have time to make anything so I hope this will do."

"Perfect. Thanks, Grace dear." Mother placed the box on the counter. "We're ready to eat. Grace, as our guest, please serve your plate from the stove, if you don't mind."

Logan beamed at Mother. She was in top form and acted as if nothing was amiss. While he consumed his fair share of the cottage pie, the joy he derived from Mother's upbeat mood and Grace's presence, were more than enough to fill his soul.

The cream-filled and chocolate-covered pastries Grace brought went down well with the tea. Mother's attitude slowly declined, and by the time Logan and Grace had stacked dishes in the dishwasher and cleaned up the kitchen, she had become silent with a blank expression on her face.

"Reg, I think Mother needs to go to bed. Will you help her?"

"Of course. After she's in bed, I'll stay upstairs with her."

"Thanks." He added a log to the fire, closed the door, and sat beside Grace.

She turned slightly toward him. Her pale pink top set off her black hair, and her dark eyes sparkled. He wanted nothing more than to hold her and declare—

"I see a Bible on the coffee table. Did you read the chapter from Matthew?"

He cleared his throat. Way to go, Grace. Introducing one topic he needed to discuss. "I did, and I have questions."

"I might have answers."

"I made notes." He opened the Bible and withdrew a sheet of paper. "Lots of points jumped out at me. Jesus encouraged us to do some things in secret and not for others to see. Giving, praying, fasting. I liked the verse about not babbling when we pray, but for us to use a few words." He glanced at her, and encouraged by her smile, kept going. "Verses 14 and 15 discuss forgiveness. I must forgive for God to forgive me. That hit home. And I love the last verse, 34. "Therefore do not worry about tomorrow for tomorrow will worry about itself. Each day has enough trouble of its own.' Oh, how I needed that admonition."

She tilted her head. "You're right. The chapter has many nuggets. I'm glad you focused on the ones you mentioned. Forgiveness is crucial to living a full life in Christ. And I agree with you about the last verse. I've learned to quit worrying. At least as much as I used to. I'm reminded of a quote on a refrigeration magnet I had once. 'Worry is like a rocking chair. It will give you something to do, but it won't get you anywhere.' How true."

"Thanks for encouraging me to read that chapter. Jesus's words have given me a lot to think about." He took her small hand in his and sighed. "I have something else to discuss."

She lowered her chin but looked at him through her lashes. "And what might that be, Dr. Quinn?"

"Well, Dr. Gentry, as you know, we are leaving Bourton tomorrow, and I want to make sure you know that I…have thoroughly enjoyed our time together and I want—" He stopped abruptly as he witnessed a small crack in her stoic façade. "Forget the 'babble'. I like you and want to continue our friendship when we get back to Texas."

"Friendship? Is that what you call it?" She pulled her hand away and crossed her arms.

"Yes." He took stock of her body language. The folded arms didn't jive with her playful facial expression. "No. More than that."

"Such as?" Again, a sliver of a smile touched her

face for a second. She was making him spell it out.

"You win, young lady. I'm falling in love with you and want to know if I should seek you out when stateside?"

"Please do, Dr. Quinn. I need some TLC."

He grinned and leaned closer as she placed her hands on his shoulders. Keeping his eyes on her lips, he set one arm around her waist, inching closer and closer, and then a knock sounded on the door. They moved apart.

"Logan." Reggie opened the door. "Irene is sleeping soundly. I'm going to make hot chocolate. Do you want any?"

Grace shook her head.

"We don't, thanks, Reg." He waited until she closed the door. "We must keep in touch."

"We can Skype."

"Good idea. I don't think we'll be in London long."

"What's the time?"

Logan checked his watch. "Nearly ten. I'll walk you home."

"Thanks. Um, I think someone followed me here this evening."

"What did he look like?"

She stood and walked through the kitchen. "Good night, Reggie." Grace stopped in the foyer and waited for Logan to help her with her coat. "It was too dark to tell much. Tall maybe, but then I think most adults are tall."

"Don't make light of it. Now, I'm going to worry about you."

"Remember the rocking chair."

He harumphed. "Yeah, but I care about you."

"I'll be careful. God gave us common sense, but it's up to us to use it. If I see the man again, I'll report him to the police." She slipped her hands into her pockets. "Besides, after you leave Bourton, I won't need to traipse through the village in the evenings."

As they walked to her house, he set his arm around her shoulders. He could have so easily picked her up and carried her. But he didn't.

At her door, she hesitated on the top stop.

Good. Now she was closer to his height. "I want to kiss you. May I?"

She grabbed his jacket, pulled him toward her, and covered his lips with hers. No matter the cold wind circling them, or the owls hooting, he was lost in the sweetness of her kiss.

CHAPTER 15

With the SUV loaded to the gills, Logan drove through Bourton-on-the-Water one last time. He'd called Grace before she set out for the dig, and they agreed to Skype later that evening.

Mother in the passenger seat, pointed out various places she and Reggie had photographed a couple of days ago. "I'm so glad we were able to stay here for so long. Logan, you've done a great job of finding quality accommodations."

"Where's our hotel in London?" Reggie asked.

"Near Hyde Park. I chose one that had parking available."

"Good." Mother adjusted her seatbelt and then turned to Logan. "Is this your car?"

He'd had the conversation many times during this trip. "No, Mother. I borrowed it from Tom Niven, my friend in Edinburgh."

"That's far away."

"It is, but he has a son in London who'll take us to the airport when we're ready to go home."

She patted his arm. "You're a good son, Logan." She looked over her shoulder into the backseat. "Isn't he, Reggie?"

"Yes. You're fortunate, Irene."

The last news Logan had of Reggie's son was unpleasant. He gambled and was always in need of money. Not Logan's problem at the moment. Settling Mother in London was paramount on his mind.

Once they were on the A40 toward Oxford, she quit commenting on their travels and rested her head as if asleep. Logan was tempted to make a detour and drive past the university, but without Grace, the visit would be flat.

He stopped in High Wycombe for a light lunch. He dreaded driving in London and had already decided to hire taxis for any travel in the city. It took him an hour to negotiate the narrow and often one-way streets to the hotel. He'd requested rooms close together. The best they could offer were rooms on the same floor. Oh, well. At least Reggie and Mother were sharing a room.

The relatively short drive had exhausted Mother. After a nap, she and Reggie asked to eat their evening meal in the hotel, which suited Logan. By bits of conversations he overheard, he noted English was not the first language for some of the waitstaff. No problem until Mother ordered nachos. The menu listed the ingredients as chili tortillas, chipotle cheese sauce, tomato salsa, guacamole, sour cream, jalapenos, and spring onions. She asked the waiter to omit the guacamole and jalapenos.

While waiting on their order, Reggie explained her method for writing her biography. Instead of describing events from her birth to the present, she was documenting slices of life she felt might be of interest to her son and two granddaughters.

The waiter deposited the classic sub sandwich in front of Reggie, the steak and ale pie with mash and veggies to Logan, and a bowl of tortilla chips for Mother. She looked up at him with a giant question mark in her expression. "Where's the rest of my nachos?"

He pointed to the bowl. "Is there."

Controlling his laughter, Logan said, "But that's just a bowl of chips. Where are the other ingredients?"

The waiter pursed his lips and looked almost as if he'd cry. He called over a suit-wearing man with a nametag. "I am the restaurant manager. What is the problem?"

Logan explained Mother didn't want the guac and jalapenos, but did want the other items.

"Oh, I see." He then spoke to the waiter in a foreign language and soon the man brought over a copy of the menu which the suit-man read. "So, madame wants the other items?"

"Yes, please."

"I'll be right back."

Minutes later, he returned with a small bowl of sour cream, another of salsa, and one of cheese. Not just any cheese. Parmesan.

Mother tried to enjoy her "meal", but she kept on blaming herself for the way she ordered or because she couldn't remember the names of things. Logan and Reggie soothed her as much as they could. She perked up a bit when Logan ordered them all bowls of chocolate ice cream, Mother's favorite. Logan noted the nachos weren't charged on the bill. He hazarded a guess that the poor waiter either received additional training in taking orders or quit his job.

In the elevator, Mother had Logan and Reggie in stitches. "Let's not go to that restaurant again. They don't know how to make nachos. If they can't get that dish right, they most certainly won't know how to make tacos. Or tamales. Or fajitas. Or—"

"Point is well taken, Mother. We won't eat there again." If they did return to the restaurant, he was sure she wouldn't remember their faux pax.

With Mother and Reggie settled in their room, Logan checked online for tickets to a musical show for the next evening. He was in luck. Not exactly good seats, but Mother's bucket list only included visiting a theater in London. Later, he took a walk into Hyde Park. The leaves crunched underfoot as he strolled along, absorbing the atmosphere. Maybe he'd bring Mother tomorrow if she felt up to the walk, especially to see the parakeets near the Peter Pan statue.

While watching the swans lazily swimming in the Serpentine, his phone buzzed. Grace on Skype. He sat on a bench facing the river and enjoyed a long chat. He told her of the nachos episode, which she found as comical as he had.

"That'll teach you to order a typical Mexican item in a fancy restaurant that has no other Mexican dishes on the menu."

"True. My steak pie was great, though. Anything interesting happen at the dig today? Have you seen the man who followed you again?"

"No sign of him. But the crew has uncovered more of the wall that extends into the mound. A few more bones."

"How much longer do you think Oxford will let you excavate?"

"I have no idea, but it makes sense for us to wrap up before the end of term."

A flock of pigeons circled overhead, landed on the embankment, and began pecking at the grass visible through the golden leaves, bobbing and cooing. "I'm taking Mother and Reggie to a musical tomorrow night. We'll be home late, so I probably won't Skype."

"That's all right."

Raindrops peltered him. "Have to go. I love you and miss you so much."

Grace gave him a big smile. "I love you."

Like juveniles, they blew kisses to each other. Logan shoved his phone into his pocket and strolled back to the hotel, oblivious to the traffic or passers-by. All that mattered was Grace reciprocated his love.

~~~

The numerous Saturday shoppers at Harrods entertained Mother as much as being in the store did. She'd always wanted to visit and was especially interested in the Food Halls. Logan had never seen such a variety of foods before. The bread smelled divine, as did the coffee.

Logan located the Coffee Bar, where they enjoyed pastries with the delicious brew. While in the Food Halls, they decided to buy takeaway meals for lunch. That selection process took over an hour as there were so many choices.

"We must buy food for Grace, too." Mother said, patting Logan's arm.

"No, Mother. She isn't in London with us."

"Why not? Did you hurt her feelings? She's very
~~~

sensitive, you know."

"I wish she were with us, but she has to work."

"Fine. I want to look at the clothes." Mother insisted on purchasing a dress to wear to the theater that evening and bought one for Reggie too. When she offered to buy Logan a tuxedo, he balked at the suggestion. The one suit he'd brought would have to do.

In the taxi on the way back to the hotel, Mother leaned close to Reggie, saying, "You haven't given me my pills today."

"Yes, I did, dear. Remember, I placed them on your little plate at breakfast and watched you swallow them."

"I remember that. What about my midday pills?"

Seated opposite the ladies, Logan frowned at Reggie. "I didn't know she took meds at midday."

"She doesn't. Only morning and evening." Reggie smiled at Mother. "You're getting mixed up. No more pills until bedtime."

If Logan didn't know better, he'd think Mother pouted.

She remained quiet for the rest of the ride, and when they alighted at the hotel, she carried her food container to her room. At the door, she turned to Logan and said, "I'll eat in my room, then I'll rest until our trip to the theater this evening."

"I'll keep my eye on her. See you later." Reggie closed the door behind her.

Head down, Logan walked to his room, the pill discussion still on his mind. Maybe Mother was confused about the schedule. She did take several prescribed meds to help slow the disease.

With time on his hands after lunch, Logan took his laptop to a quiet seating area off the lobby and checked his email. Wayne Hammond informed him Adrian Kerns was adamant about appealing his sentence. Logan better be prepared to defend himself when he returned to Texas. Just what he needed. More legal issues to cloud his already damaged reputation.

All dressed in their finery, Logan escorted Mother and Reggie to the taxi. The ride to the theater didn't take long. He wouldn't have darkened the doors for anyone else and was rewarded by Mother's excitement during the musical performance.

She enjoyed the show but the late night took its toll and she fell asleep in the taxi. When they reached the hotel, she was agitated and in a high state of confusion. Logan helped her to her room, and while she changed into her nightgown in the bathroom, he waited by the window. Reggie sat in the armchair in the corner of the room.

Mother emerged and stood beside her bed, but shrugged and chewed her upper lip. "What must I do?"

Logan had already pulled down the duvet. He fluffed the pillows and took her hand. "Come, Mother. Get into bed and I'll make sure you're snug and warm."

She sat on the bed, shaking her head. "This isn't my room, Logan."

"Yes, it is, Mother. Your room in the hotel. Remember, we're in London."

"Okay. I'm tired." She slid her legs onto the bed and lay down. "Don't forget to invite Grace to breakfast."

Logan covered her and kissed her forehead. "I won't." *If only she was in the hotel with us.*

"Goodnight, Mother. I love you."

She snuggled into the pillows and smiled. "Please stay with me until I'm asleep."

"Of course." Logan sat on the side of the bed and watched her drift off. There' be no trips to Dover or Brighton. Time to take her home. "See you tomorrow, Reg. Thanks for all you do for her." Although he paid Regina for her help, she always went above and beyond expectations.

Given the late hour, Logan texted Grace.

Goodnight, my love. I'm very concerned about Mother. I'll make our fight reservations tomorrow. See you stateside soon.

CHAPTER 16

Saddened by the deterioration in Irene's condition, Grace said a special prayer for her that morning in church. She also repeated her plea for Logan to rekindle his desire to follow Christ. His insightful review of the chapter in Matthew gave her a sneak peek into his analytical mind. If their relationship developed further, she could see herself enjoying many lively discussions in the future.

Flushed by the direction her thoughts were taking, Grace declined an invitation to lunch from an elderly couple. "I need to get back to the dig site. But I appreciate the offer." She hurried to the house, changed clothes, and chomped on a day-old sandwich while she strode to the dig. Autumn had arrived in full force, bringing gusty winds along with lower temperatures.

At the site, Marcus hailed her to Tertius. "What are you doing here? Why aren't you taking off the rest of the day?"

"All my laundry is done, and reports are up to date. There's nowhere else I'd rather be."

"We uncovered more of the wall and found a few bones, but I can't decide if they belong to the teenager or not."

He went with her to the tent where the bones were laid out on the table. Grace examined several. "You're correct. At least one adult. I'll have to examine them more closely."

"Yeah. I agree, but I kept all the bones together for now."

"Hey, Marcus and Grace. Come look." Kristy called from the site.

Grace followed Marcus out of the tent and hurried to the site on the mound.

Grinning, Kristy held a small object in her hand. "It's a hair comb, but not made from bone."

"An interesting find." Grace looked at the item. "Clean it up a bit more, and then you tell us what you think. What material was used and when was it made?"

"Thanks, prof. I'll work on it."

Susan mumbled under her breath and pulled off her gloves. "I also helped in that area, Dr. Gentry." She climbed out of the hole and stomped off toward the tent.

"It's my experience where there's one piece of jewelry, there'll be more. Keep digging, team." Grace deliberately used that word and hoped Susan heard. For the first time at the site, Grace picked up a trowel and brush from the container and began moving dirt close to the exposed wall. Her time to teach her students was fast drawing to a close and she wanted to get her hands dirty before Peggy shut down the site. And with no Logan to visit or cottage living room to snuggle in, she had to occupy her time.

She'd enjoyed her time in Oxford, but her return to Texas couldn't come soon enough. However, she had a major problem. If she wasn't offered the job at UT, how was she going to earn a living? For once, her heart and head agreed. She loved Logan and would live wherever he settled. That might restrict her choice of employment. Maybe she could work at a garden center. After all, she knew a lot about soil and could dig holes with tiny shovels.

Her trowel hit something more substantial than gravel. Grace removed small bits of dirt and then brushed away more grains. A small oval object. More brushing revealed a brooch about the size of an egg. Even with remnants of the earth still clinging to it, Grace recognized a mother-of-pearl cameo within a gold frame with a clasp on the back.

Resting on her haunches, she frowned as she stared at the exquisite example of Victorian craftsmanship. The profile of a woman with flowers carved into her lavish tresses. Grace stood and exited the hole. "Kristy, come to the tent, please."

Susan, who had returned to the site minutes before, glared at her crew mate.

Artifact in hand, Kristy followed Grace. "I don't think this is very old. I've removed as much dirt as I can. Two tines of the comb are broken, and a few of the tiny jewels in the crest are missing. What do you think the material is, Dr. Gentry?"

Taking the comb, Grace touched the fine tines. "It's tortoise shell. Not plastic imitation, but the real deal."

"You mean people used shells from real tortoises? How cruel."

"They did, but—this won't placate your soft heart—they killed the tortoise first, then removed the shell and boiled it until soft and pliable."

"Terrible. I'd rather use the plastic kind. How old is it?"

"Probably Victorian. Same as the cameo I found." Grace held out the brooch.

"Ooh, that's lovely. How did these items end up in our Anglo-Saxon burial site?"

"I don't know. Let's keep our find to ourselves for now. Okay? We don't want another unwelcome visitor."

"I understand."

"Tell the others to bring all the bones they found so we can secure them in tubs. We've all worked hard and deserve a break." Grace found a small plastic bag and placed the comb and brooch inside. She'd keep them safe in her pocket for now and then hide them in her suitcase back at the house.

Marcus and Charles carried the few bones they'd found and placed them with the others. "Should we put them all in one tub?"

"For now, yes." Grace poked her head out of the tent, looking for Susan. She stood on the rim of the excavation and gazed at the lake. "Susan, please come help with the bones."

Taking small, slow steps, Susan reached the tent and rolled her eyes at Grace. "I'm sorry I pouted. But it seems Kristy is your favorite and I'm jealous."

Grace guided Susan away from the tent. "She is not my favorite, but she certainly works hard." She let that statement sink in for a few seconds.

"I do, too." Twirling a strand of her long dark hair,

the student raised a brow "Well, I do most of the time. I…I want to find something significant."

"Maybe you will tomorrow. Please help the guys pack the bones in the tub."

"All right. As long as I don't have to help Charles."

Aha. Susan must still be smarting after he broke up with her. However, she had been reminded to keep her personal problems separate from the work.

Alone outside the tent, Grace paced to the lake embankment and stopped. The hair on the back of her neck prickled. She turned slowly toward the parking area. A man stood there, hands on his hips. He might have been the same guy who followed her.

A shiver snaked along her shoulders and down her spine. She was right to ask Kristy to keep their find a secret. In the mood Susan was in, she might blab to anyone who paid her attention.

CHAPTER 17

Banging on his door jolted Logan awake. He'd fallen asleep while reading his email. He scooted back the desk chair and stepped to the door which he pulled open.

"Logan, Irene has gone. I can't find her anywhere." Panic raced across Reggie's face.

"What? When?" Logan couldn't form a complete sentence.

"She wanted to nap after lunch, so I went to the gift shop once she was settled in bed." Her lips quivered. "I was only gone for half an hour at most."

"Where have you looked?"

"Only our room. I...I..."

"Okay. I'll go down to the restaurant and I'll check with the concierge. Did she take anything with her? Coat, purse?"

"No. Both are in the closet."

"Since she doesn't have a keycard, please stay in your room in case she returns. I'll call if I find her downstairs." Logan grabbed his cell and keycard and hurried to the elevator. He should have realized something was amiss when Mother didn't even ask to go to church that morning.

She wasn't in the restaurant or the bar. The concierge hadn't seen her leave the hotel, but Logan checked outside anyway. No sign of her on the sidewalk. What else could he do?

Back inside, the concierge stopped him. "Sir, I will ask our housekeeping staff to look for her. I'm sure she didn't leave our facility."

"Thank you. That will be helpful. We need to check the pubic bath, um, restrooms, too."

"Yes, sir. I will tell them. Please give me your cell phone number so I can contact you if we find her."

Logan provided the information. "Thank you." He didn't know what else to do, except the one thing he hadn't done in many years. He prayed. *God, please help us find her.*

Although the staff was searching conference rooms, restrooms, and the kitchen, Logan did his fair share of opening doors to public areas and calling for her. His heart squeezed tight in his chest, and his mind focused on the worst-case scenarios, he searched from floor to floor and even checked the roof access. No sight of Mother.

He phoned Reggie. "Any sign?"

"Noting. I've propped open our door and will call if she comes."

Minutes dragged by as if they rode in a vehicle on the Katy Freeway in Houston during rush hour traffic. Logan descended the stairs and reached the seventh floor when the concierge called him.

"Sir, Mrs. Quinn has been located. Please come to

the fifth floor. She is seated by the lift and is waiting for you."

Blowing out a massive breath, Logan ran down the two flights and rushed to the elevator. Mother sat, arms folded, conversing with a member of staff.

"Hi, Mother." He hoped his tone was as normal as possible.

"Logan, where have you been?"

"Looking for you—"

She stood and spread her arms wide. "Here I am." She then twirled around and around.

Logan stopped her before she became giddy. "Let's go to your room. Reggie's waiting for you." He looked at the housekeeper and mouthed, "Thank you."

"That's odd. Reggie told me to meet Grace on the fifth floor. That's why I'm here. I know my room is on six," Mother said as she entered the elevator.

"But Grace is in Bourton."

She nodded. "That's what I told Reggie. I don't like her anymore. She doesn't want to go to my favorite village."

Standing beside her, he shook his head. What was she talking about?

By the time she reached her room, Mother had forgotten what she'd said about Reggie and greeted her like a long-lost friend. "There you are. I was waiting for you by the elevator."

Logan shook his head again and closed the door. "Yes, she was one floor down, on fifth."

"Come sit beside me, dear." Reggie drew her to the bed. "Do you want to take a nap?"

"Nope. I want to go to Bourton-on-the-Water."

Logan walked to the window and stared at the busy

street below. No telling what would have happened if Mother had gone outside. *She is safe. Thank you, Lord.* He turned and noted the expectant expression on Mother's face. "We spent two weeks in Bourton. Remember, we stayed in the cottage with the conservatory and the pretty garden."

"I want to go back." She stood and stepped toward Logan. "Please." She grabbed his shirt and said through clenched teeth, "I must go back."

"Okay, Mother. Why?" Not anticipating a rational reply, he placed his hands over hers, and she relaxed her grip.

"I want to talk to Nigel."

Definitely an unexpected response. "Nigel?"

"Yes. I have to apologize to him for my attitude and Grandfather Gee's, um, ignoring his grandmother and their son." She glanced around the room. Her train of thought jumped the rails. "Oh, there's my bed. Nap time. Make plans, please, Logan." Back on track, but she lay down and pulled the duvet over her body.

He shrugged at Reggie. "Has she been talking about Bourton a lot?"

Reggie motioned for him to join her in the small sitting area. "She has, but I tried to convince her we'd been there already."

"Did she mention Nigel?"

"Yes, but—"

"I think she has a legitimate need to see him. I'd want to apologize too if it was my grandfather." And besides, he'd see Grace again. "I'll arrange another visit to Bourton, and then I think it will be time to return to Texas. You okay with that?"

"Of course." She walked with him to the door.

"And I won't leave Irene alone again. Sorry for scaring you."

"Something Mother said is bothering me." He looked directly at Reggie. "She said you told her Grace was on the fifth floor."

The woman harrumphed and frowned. "Why would I do that? Irene's getting more and more confused. I understand it's the disease, but I'm tired of being blamed for…her mishaps."

"I'm not blaming you." At this point, Logan had to believe Reggie. He peeked at Mother before he left the room. "I'll let you know about the village arrangements." He first went downstairs and thanked the concierge for the staff's help. Once back in his room, he checked online for cottage rentals in Bourton. Even near the end of October, there were few available. Finally, he found a three-bedroom, two-bathroom cottage that had a late cancelation.

Puffitts. Mother would love the name and the front and back gardens. The online photos convinced him to book the place for a week.

~~~

Usually, Mother relied on Reggie to help her pack. That morning, however, she was ready to leave the hotel when Logan entered their room.

"Let's go, son. Please ask Nigel to come visit as soon as we get there."

Logan laughed and grabbed her suitcase handle. "I will, Mother, but remember he might be busy."

Luggage loaded, he drove out of London with the assistance of the Satnav system. Without it, he wouldn't have dared drive in the UK. With a three o'clock check-in at the cottage, Logan had to be creative to use up
~~~

four hours and to keep Mother mollified. High Wycombe was about halfway, and he stopped there again for lunch.

After ordering, he went to the restroom, and on his return, he was sure he saw Mother accept something from Reggie, which she put in her mouth and swallowed with a drink of water.

"Did Mother just take her medication?"

Reggie's brows rose. "No, you must be mistaken."

"Mother, are you all right?"

"Of course, son. I'm eager to get back on the road."

"Did you just take some pills?"

"Nope." She sipped her water. "Just thirsty, is all."

With that reply, he had to be satisfied, but he'd keep a close watch on what meds she *did* take.

Mother barely ate, and no matter how many times Logan reminded her they didn't have to hurry because they couldn't check in until three, she wanted to get back in the car.

To use up more time, he consulted his map and made a detour from Oxford and took the A44 highway to Moreton-in-Marsh. Figuring Mother might be hungry, he stopped at a restaurant in Chipping Norton. "I'm thirsty. Who's in the mood for tea and cream scones?" He knew the invitation would tempt her.

"Oh, yes. Yum." She latched onto his arm and strode beside him into the café. "Are we getting close to Bourton?"

"Yes, Mother." He pulled out a chair for her, did the same for Reggie, and then joined them at the small round table.

Tea for three and scones with the prerequisite

strawberry jam and clotted cream were delivered to their table in record time. Logan tried to eat slowly, but the delicacies were too tasty.

Appetites satiated and minutes eaten up, they returned to the vehicle, and Logan drove on to Moreton-in-Marsh, then south to Bourton.

Puffitts was situated on Lansdowne Road, west of the village center. Logan eased off the highway onto the road and parked in front of the cottage.

As soon as Mother saw the front garden, she was intrigued. "Logan, how beautiful. Look, an arch for the roses, and wisteria by the front door. And a birdfeeder. Oh, my. This is lovely."

Reggie climbed the steps to the gravel pathway. "Even in the fall, the garden is a delight."

After carrying the suitcases inside, Logan chose the single downstairs bedroom. The ladies had double bedrooms upstairs and could share the large bathroom which had a tub and shower.

Mother unpacked quickly and then bombarded him in his room.

"Please call Nigel now." She sat on the bed. "This is a cute room. Mine's very nice, too. I like this cottage, son."

He sat beside her and made the call.

"Good afternoon. Wayfarer's Inn."

Logan recognized the voice but asked anyway, "Is this Nigel Stewart?"

"Speaking. Logan?"

"Yes, hello."

"How is Irene? Are you back in the States?"

"No. We went to London but returned to Bourton."

"That's interesting."

"Mother insisted. She, um, would like to meet you again."

She patted his knee and grinned.

"I'd like that too. When?"

"As soon as you can manage it. Or we could go to Stow." Logan looked at Mother. She frowned and shook her head. "Sorry, she just nixed that idea. When can you come here?"

"Mornings are better for me. How about ten o'clock tomorrow?"

"Perfect. Thanks for understanding. See you then."

Mother tugged on his sleeve. "What did he say?"

"Tomorrow at ten."

"Thank you, son. I'm glad he can come here. I don't want to meet his family. It'll be too humiliating." She stood and left the room, stopping in the kitchen. "I like this cottage. Do you want some tea?"

Logan had followed her. "Yes, please. Look, here's a welcome basket. With cookies."

"No, no, Logan. They are biscuits." She playfully slapped his arm. "Haven't you learned anything since being in England?"

Reggie entered from the living room. "How can you two want more tea so soon after our stop in Chipping Norton?"

Mother checked her watch. "It is teatime, Reggie."

"Well, I don't want any, thanks. I'm going to see the back garden. Care to join me, Irene?"

The women left the kitchen, and Logan made tea for two. Mother had a collection of teabags she'd bought during their travels. He set a box on the counter and removed two bags. Hot tea hadn't replaced coffee as his beverage of choice, at least in the mornings, but he'd grown accustomed to the taste and the ritual.

Mother returned to the kitchen, claiming it was cold outside, and asked Logan to start the fire. He carried the tea tray into the living room and lit the already stacked wood in the grate.

"Thanks, son. I like these biscuits." Mother drank her tea and nibbled the cookies while snuggling under a soft blanket on the bright fuchsia sofa. The drive and the anticipated meeting with Nigel probably tired her out, so she soon retreated upstairs to take a nap.

When Reggie came inside, she also went upstairs. Logan was sure she didn't want to be left alone with him. Oh, well. If she were tired of her duties, they'd be over soon. In a week or less.

Confident Mother was asleep, and Reggie was watching out for her, he drove to Sherborne Street. Puffitts was a little further from Grace's house. He hadn't told her of their return and waited for the white Oxford van. With the onset of dusk, he expected the vehicle any minute. When Marcus parked in the driveway, Logan stayed in the SUV until Grace and the crew were in the house. He knocked on the door, and when Grace opened it, he said, "Surprise."

She gasped. "What are you doing here?"

Not the welcome he hoped for.

"Sorry, Logan. That was rude." She jumped down the two steps and into his arms.

He hugged her, set her down, and kissed her like he hadn't seen her for weeks. "Mother demanded we return to Bourton. I wasn't about to deny her the privilege."

"Come inside." She drew him in and closed the door. "Is Irene all right?"

"More confused more frequently, but otherwise, fine."

"You should have let me know you were coming. I have plans for the evening I can't change."

"No problem. I'll spend time with you tomorrow, if I may." He played with a strand of her hair.

"Certainly. We've made some interesting discoveries. But right now, I have to shower and change. I'm meeting the head of the Cotswold Archeological Trust for supper in Cirencester."

"I won't keep you. It's so good to see you." He leaned close and whispered, "And hold you."

She blushed and waited for Marcus to close the living room door. "Kiss me, then I have to go."

"My pleasure."

CHAPTER 18

Prepared tea tray set on the kitchen counter, a welcoming fire in the living room, and Mother pacing a rut in the carpet. She asked again, "Logan, what time is Nigel coming?"

"Ten o'clock, Mother. Fifteen more minutes. Why don't you sit down and relax?"

"I can't." She entered the kitchen and examined the tray. "These biscuits and pastries look nice. Did you make them?"

Logan laughed and set his arm around her shoulders. "Oh, Mother, dear. You don't want me anywhere near an oven or cake pans or cookie sheets. Give me a grill any time and I'll prepare a fantastic meal."

She frowned. "Then, who made these?"

"I bought them at the bakery this morning."

"That was a good idea. I'll wait in the living room." She sat on the sofa, legs crossed and hands in her lap. "Will he like me, son?"

Seated beside her, Logan took her in his arms.

"Yes, Mother. He will like you. Don't fret." A car door slammed, and footsteps crunched on the gravel. "He's here." Logan stepped to the door and opened it. "Welcome, Nigel. Please come in."

The visitor removed his coat and hung it on the banister. "Hello, Irene, Logan. "I'm so glad you asked to see me."

Mother rose and held out her hand.

After shaking hands, Nigel hesitated.

"Sit beside Mother. I'll take the armchair." After discussing matters with her earlier, Logan had a spiel and questions ready in case she forgot why her cousin came. But he needn't have worried.

She cleared her throat. "First of all, Nigel, I need to apologize for my attitude when we first met. It was a shock to learn about Grandfather Gee's affair."

"I can understand that."

"When we get back to Texas, I will send you photographs of him, and I'd like to keep in touch." Mother looked at Logan. "What else did I want to say?"

He had reminders at the ready. "You think your grandfather knew about his English son."

"That's right. Since meeting you, I've reviewed memories of the man. He often visited these villages and I came with him frequently. One time I met a young boy named George, a few years older than me. Grandfather was angry that we'd spoken and wanted to be pen pals."

Nigel shrugged. "Although George is a common name, that boy couldn't have been his son."

"I know. Maybe he thought his son had a son and also named him George."

"Possible. The English like to use family names

generation after generation. Except my parents. They just liked the name Nigel."

"Grandfather Gee might have been getting senile. Years later, when I told him I was marrying George, the boy I'd met that day in… Where, Logan?"

"Broadway."

"Yes, in Broadway. He had a stroke. I'm sure he thought I was going to marry a relative."

Mother seemed to have exhausted her set of questions and smiled at Logan. "Is it teatime yet?"

"I'll put the kettle on." Where was Reggie when he needed her? Probably still upstairs. After breakfast, she'd given him all Mother's medications, prescription bottles, and the weekly container. Her reason—she felt he didn't trust her anymore. He hadn't realized his doubts had been so obvious.

Tea made, he carried in the tray and set it on the coffee table. He still had items to discuss with Nigel, but he waited until they'd enjoyed the tea and edibles and contributed to the small talk.

"Mother does have a few other things to add." She gazed into the fire, so Logan spoke for her. "She's sorry your grandfather didn't help your grandmother financially. There's not a lot she can do about it now, but she—"

She held up a hand to Logan. "I'm angry and disappointed at the man for what he did or rather didn't do for your grandmother. His behavior was disgraceful. He wasn't wealthy, but he could have provided for her and his son. I'm ashamed."

Nigel set his empty cup on the table. "I'm sure she might have felt that way at first, but she later married and led a good life. Edward and Doris didn't have any children, and he accepted George Henry as his own."

"I'm relieved to hear that." Mother set her cup down, too, leaned back, and folded her arms.

Logan asked about Nigel's family, but Mother seemed oblivious to their conversation. She plucked at folds in her pants, brushed crumbs off her sweater, and gazed around the room as if not sure where she was.

Nigel might have recognized the symptoms too. He shrugged and stood.

His action seemed to coerce her back to the present. She smiled and looked up at him. "I'm glad you came, Nigel. Give my love to your family."

"I will. And I'll write." He glanced at Logan. "Or we can email if that's more convenient."

"Yeah. Mother no longer has an account, but I'll share your communications with her." Logan handed him a card on which he'd written his email address.

"I look forward to receiving the photographs. Thank you, Irene." He hugged her, picked up his coat, and left the house.

Mother chomped on another cookie and asked, "Who was that nice man, Logan?"

Mission accomplished, she easily slipped back into confusion. "He was a friend. Would you like to go for a walk in the village?"

"Yes. Down by the river." And back to reality.

Logan called up the stairs, "Reg, we're going for a walk. Want to join us?"

"Sure. I'll be right down."

They strolled into the village and sat beside the river for a while. Mother and Reggie talked about their school days and Logan enjoyed the contributions Mother made. At times, she was as mentally healthy as ever and even surprised him with events she remembered. Then, in a blink, she forgot where she was.

"I'm hungry, son. Take me to H. E. B., please, so I can buy groceries."

H. E. B., their grocery store of choice back in Texas. "How about we have lunch at that restaurant across the street? They serve great fish and ships."

"Even better. I don't want to cook, anyway." Irene stood and set off.

He caught up with her as she was about to cross the street in front of a car.

Seated at a corner table, they placed their order. Logan didn't want to antagonize Reggie further and made a point of including her in the conversation while they ate.

Back at the cottage, he helped Mother upstairs for her nap and asked Reggie to watch out for her. Eager to see Grace, he drove to the dig. The white van in the parking area was a welcome sight. He walked toward the slight mound where the crew were working.

Grace stood on the rim of the hole and turned at his approach. "Good afternoon. All well at the cottage?"

"Yes." He veiled his desire to hold her and kiss her. Instead, he described the meeting with Nigel. "Seems my great grandfather didn't acknowledge his son, nor did he help financially. Nigel doesn't hold any grudges, and I'm glad he and Mother parted on good terms." He helped her down from the small mound. "How'd your meeting go in Cirencester?"

"Fine. I think the Archeological Trust wanted to make sure we weren't disturbing the Hilltop Fort area, and only excavating close to the lakes. I reassured him on both issues."

He pointed to the four students working in the hole. "Found anything exciting?"

"We have." She drew him toward the tent and then stopped and glanced at Susan and Charles who were arguing. They quit when they noticed her. Grace rolled her eyes. "Two artifacts. Kristy found a tortoiseshell comb, and I uncovered a cameo brooch. The others know she found a comb, but I'm keeping the cameo a secret for now. The pieces are Victorian, and the bones are not ancient. I don't want word to get out that we've located a nineteenth-century burial site."

"That's interesting. May I see the pieces?"

"Not yet. I hid them at the house. Susan is disillusioned and might gossip."

"I understand. Can you come for supper tonight? I know Mother will be happy to see you. She often asked about you while we were in London."

Grace grinned. "At least someone in the family missed me."

"Whoa, I missed you. And I told you that every time we Skyped."

She pulled him into the tent. "You missed me? Show me how much."

He kissed her deeply and only moved apart when he heard a voice outside.

Marcus called, "Dr. Gentry."

Grace ran a hand through Logan's hair, then stepped aside. "Come in. What's up?"

Lifting the flap, he said, "We found an interesting item."

"Thanks, Marcus. I'll be right there."

After he left, she added, "I have to go. See you this

evening."

"I'll pick you up since Puffitts is further from the house."

"Okay. About six?"

"Yup."

They exited the tent together. Grace hurried to the mound while Logan walked to his car. Head down and daydreaming about proposing to Grace and her getting the job in Austin and…

He shoved his hands into his pockets and looked up. A man circled the van but ran down the hiking trail as soon as he noticed Logan. Not a coincidence. He phoned Grace.

She whispered, "Miss me already?"

"No. Yes. Is the van locked?"

"Of course. Why?"

"A man was loitering in the parking area. He seemed particularly interested in the van."

"I'll have Marcus drive it closer to our tent. Sir Barrette will understand."

"Please be careful when you leave this evening, my love." He desperately wanted to return to the site and protect her himself.

"I will. We will. I think we should keep the tubs of bones in the house overnight."

"Good idea. Especially the more recent finds. See you later." Logan walked along the hiking trail for a bit, but the loiterer was probably long gone. As he drove away, he wished for the first time that Mother did not need him. The selfish thought only lasted a few seconds. How could he keep Grace safe and help Mother at the same time? He couldn't do it alone. *Please, dear God, keep Grace and the crew safe.*

CHAPTER 19

Beyond the wall section the team had uncovered so far, Charles had found a leather pouch, about four inches by six. Machine stitching along the edges of the folded-over flap determined it was not Anglo-Saxon.

"Is there anything in it?" Grace asked.

Charles patted the pouch. "Nothing solid."

"There might be papers inside. Let's open it in the tent, and I think it's time for another lesson." Grace led the way. "Charles, since you found the artifact, set it on the table and carefully lift the flap."

He complied, bending over the table. "It's empty. Except for grains of sand."

"What do you think it might have been used for?" Grace looked at the students, briefly making eye contact with Kristy.

She said, "Jewelry?"

"Possibly. Other suggestions?"

"Money. It's not big enough for much else." Susan touched the leather. "It's not very old."

"I agree with Susan regarding the age of the pouch. Now, let's discuss the bones we located in this part of Tertius." Anticipating this lesson, Grace had asked Marcus to bring in the tub containing the bones of the male they'd found in Primus. She removed the lid and lifted out a femur which she placed beside a femur found in Tertius. "One of these bones is hundreds of years old. One is not. Can we estimate the age of bones by just a visual examination? If so, what should we look for?"

"Color." Kristy gave the first answer.

"Broken or chipped ends," Susan added.

"Signs of weathering and overall degradation." Charles's contribution.

Marcus rubbed his chin. "Contextual clues. We know a lot about the Primus and Secundus digs from previous excavations and the history of the area. The mound where Tertius is located was probably not connected to the inhabitants of centuries ago. Dr. Gentry, you never did tell us about the comb Kristy found. That might help us identify the age of the bones."

"You are so right, Marcus. Everyone gave good answers. Of course, we can postulate the bones from Primus and Secundus are from the Anglo-Saxon period." Grace thought about discussing the cameo but decided not to. "The comb Kristy found is made from tortoiseshell, and I estimate it to be from the Victorian age. The leather pouch might be from the same period. Can we make the assumption the bones are too?"

The students looked at each other, but no one seemed ready to make a committed statement.

"Congratulations, y'all," she grinned and added,

"you all. No, we cannot make that assumption just by a visual inspection. I can positively say the bones are not old enough to be Anglo-Saxon, and they do not appear to be recent, as in this century. The sophisticated technology at Oxford will provide more accurate dates. In the meantime, we keep working into the mound. Tomorrow. It's getting late. Let's pack all the tubs back in the van and when we get to the house, they must be taken inside for protection."

Thankful there were two bathrooms at the house, Grace hurried into one and showered. Pink sweater and black pants donned, she waited in the living room for Logan. By now the crew knew she and Logan were an item and refrained from teasing her.

As on previous occasions, she enjoyed the meal and the company. While they had tea and biscuits around the fire in the living room, Grace paid close attention to Irene. She seldom spoke during the evening and constantly looked at Logan. He anticipated many of her needs, and Grace loved him for his sensitivity toward his mother. The woman was slipping fast. Grace wouldn't be surprised if Logan decided to return to Texas any day. She hung her head. If she'd had a mother like Irene, she would have taken special care of her, too.

Grace hadn't interacted much with Reggie during the time she'd visited Cloisters. The woman seemed extra quiet, even subdued. After Reggie took Irene upstairs, Grace snuggled beside Logan on the sofa. "Your mother has changed so much since the first day I met her."

He rested his head on Grace's. "She has. I'm not sure how long we'll stay here. I booked Puffitts for a week, but…"

"I understand. What about Reggie? Is she all right?"

"I think she's tiring of her responsibilities." He sighed. "Enough about those women. I want to kiss the woman in my arms."

"What's stopping you?"

~~~

Dense early morning fog shrouded the dig site as Marcus drove up to the tent. Grace imagined Roman soldiers might appear any moment and demand the interlopers leave. She grinned and opened the van door. "Rain is forecast for later today, so let's work as long as we can." Huddled in her coat, she entered the tent and spread a cloth on the table, ready for any bones they might find.

The crew worked for hours and found nothing then Susan hollered, "Dr. Gentry. Come quickly. I found something."

The note of excitement in her voice amused Grace. She remembered her first find and hurried to the mound.

"Look." Susan held a small object in her gloved hand. "A buckle."

Grace climbed the mound and took the object. A brief examination and she knew the results would disappoint Susan. "Brush off more dirt and then you tell us about it."

Beaming, Susan delicately removed the soil. Soon, her smile was replaced by a frown. "It's…it's plastic. Hard, black plastic. Attached to a piece of a belt." She dropped the buckle as if it were covered in roaches.

In an attempt to mollify Susan, Grace picked up
~~~

the object. "This is not Victorian as the other finds might be but it's still relevant. Why?"

"People might have tossed rubbish here." Charles gave an obvious answer.

"Yeah, and then it was trodden underfoot or deliberately buried," Marcus added.

"We found the bones down two meters, but the buckle and the pouch were located at one meter." Kristy adjusted the cap on her curls. "In my estimation, the bones and the artifacts are not from the same period."

That girl was going places. "You are absolutely correct, Kristy. They might be connected, but I doubt it. Let's focus on the area where we found the pouch and the buckle. I think it's attached to a piece of webbing, you know like a belt or strap. Leave the bones for another time. Once they are dated at Oxford, if the powers that be want to excavate further, they'll know where to dig."

Although two canopies protected Tertius, the gentle rain hampered the crew's work. At noon, Grace called a halt to operations. "A quick reminder—please don't tell anyone what we've found. I told you about the man who followed me last week and the guy Logan noticed by the van. They seem a bit too interested in our work."

Tubs secure in the van, Marcus drove back to the residence.

"I know it's a pain to transfer the tubes to and from the house every day. Thanks for understanding," Grace said to the crew.

They decided to eat in the village, but Grace made a sandwich and documented the latest finds. Kristy's conclusion was spot on. The few bones they'd found had no connection to the artifacts. What did the cameo, the comb, the pouch, and the buckle have in common? Two items of jewelry or at least adornment, a pouch where they might have been kept. But the buckle didn't seem to fit in. Maybe they'd find a connection when they returned to the site.

Reports written, Grace began compiling her end-of-year evaluations. Sure, they weren't due for several weeks, but she wanted to include the contributions the students made to the excavations while fresh on her mind.

Massaging her stiff neck muscles hours later, she sighed. Now, to get ready for Logan who was going to pick her up again for supper at Puffitts. Seated in the living room with Kristy and Marcus twenty minutes later, Grace joined in the chit-chat while checking the time every few minutes. He was late. Six-fifteen. She phoned him but he didn't answer. Odd. Maybe something had happened to Irene.

"Marcus, I'm taking the van. Okay?"

"Sure. Drive carefully and enjoy yourself."

Cloudy skies enhanced the dusk and streetlights were already shining. Grace noticed another vehicle in the parking area in front of the cottage and pulled in along the street. As she passed the other car, she did a double take. Had she seen it in the lot by the dig site? Prickles crawled across her shoulders. She walked toward the front door, careful to keep her footsteps from crunching the gravel. The top half of the stable door with clear glass panels was ajar. Most unusual since cold-natured Irene wouldn't want nippy air to dilute the warmth from the fire. The outside light wasn't on, but lights in the living room revealed the occupants.

Logan stood with his back to the bay window, a man leaned against the wall beside the fireplace, a splash of color from Reggie's clothes indicated she sat on the chair nearest the kitchen, and Irene perched on the sofa. Another man paced behind her.

The prickling sensation persisted. Grace crept closer and crouched by the door, out of sight. Faint voices reached her. She turned up the volume of her hearing aids and didn't like what she heard.

A man's voice, "We've been following your little friend from Oxford. She often visited you at the other cottage and now she comes here. Right?"

Logan grunted, "Yes."

"Well, tell her and her people to stop digging. Hasn't that site been disturbed enough?"

He must be local to know about the vast excavations done in the past.

"Why should I tell her?"

"Because we could so easily hurt her. Or your mother."

Irene squealed.

"Take that knife away from my mother."

"Try and make me. See if I'm serious or not."

Two men up to no good. Grace could contact the cops but they were too far away to be of any instant help. Besides saying a quick prayer, she had to do something.

Rising slowly, she peeked through the glass. Sure enough, one of the thugs leaned over seated Irene with a knife to her throat. The other shorter man also wielding a knife, hovered by the fire.

Grace's action must have caught Logan's attention.

He briefly glanced at her through the bay window, then frowned and made a subtle movement with his hand as if to warn her off. "Okay. Okay. I'll tell her to stop digging, but please, leave my mother alone."

"Yeah." Same voice. He must be in charge. "Tell your friend in the pink coat to go home. To make sure you do, your mother is coming with me." He grabbed Irene's arm and pulled her up.

Logan attempted to lunge forward but the younger man barred his way, knife at the ready.

Grace had to act. She couldn't let them take Irene away. She did a quick inventory of her surroundings. Bricks edged the gravel path. She pried one loose then chanced another peek. The intruder backstepped toward the door with his left arm around Irene's neck, and the knife presumably in his right hand.

Logan said, "If you're taking her outside, she needs her coat."

"Not where we're going." He moved his right hand and pointed the knife at Logan. "Stay back."

Grace's cue. She pushed open the top half of the door and used the brick to whack him on the side of his head, the best blow she could deliver given her position.

The would-be kidnapper stumbled sideways, releasing Irene as he stuck out his arm to catch himself. The knife dropped from his hand and when he spied Grace, he opened the bottom half of the door and ran out, leaving behind a strong whiff of body odor.

In an instant, Logan knelt beside Irene who'd fallen forward onto the sofa arm.

The other man hesitated. Bad decision. Reggie picked up a poker from beside the fireplace and hit him across his back. He also dropped his knife, dashed past Grace, and disappeared into the night.

"Mother, are you all right? Did he hurt you?" Logan eased her up and onto the sofa.

Irene shook her head. "I'm fine, but I don't like those men, son. Who were they?"

He stayed at her feet and chuckled. "We don't have to worry about them. Grace chased them away."

She dropped the brick, her hand shaking, and locked the front door before staggering to the sofa and slumping onto the plush cushions.

"Grace, are you all right?" Logan placed his hand on her knee.

"I…think so."

"You took a big risk. Thank you."

Breathing in large gulps of air, she only shrugged. Yeah, so much could have gone wrong when she acted, but praise the Lord, her plan worked.

Reggie set the poker back with the other andirons and stepped toward the kitchen. "I'll make us all some nice tea."

Grace giggled, then reared back and laughed.

"What's so funny?" Logan asked, no humor in his voice.

"Reggie has picked up the wonderful English habit of handling every event, happy or traumatic, by putting on the kettle. I'm surprised she didn't also say, 'I'll add lots of sugar.'"

CHAPTER 20

At breakfast the next morning, Mother exhibited no ill effects from the previous evening's event. The police had arrived within the hour and gathered descriptions of the men, their clothing, and details about their vehicle. After they'd secured the knives for fingerprints, and ascertained Mother didn't require medical attention, they'd left with assurances they'd keep Logan and Grace informed about the investigation.

By noon, he decided he could visit the dig site and leave Mother in Reggie's care. The woman's attitude had undergone a remarkable one-eighty since the thugs' visit. Logan drove to the site and hurried down the path toward the tent. He hugged Grace in full view of the crew, and she didn't object.

"Is Irene okay?" Grace slid her arms around his waist.

"Yes. And you? I still can't believe what you did."

"I'm fine. Any word from the police?"

"Not yet. What did your boss say?"

"Dr. Wilson left the decision to go or stay up to me. I want to continue the excavation of the mound. There must be something there those men don't want us to find."

"I can understand your desire to keep digging, but I wish you'd reconsider. I'll be returning to Texas soon and can't keep you safe."

Grace chuckled. "Your sentiment is comforting, but this is my job." She stepped away from him and shoved her hands into her pockets. "I have faith the police will be able to arrest the two intruders. They each left knives with their fingerprints. And you recognized the burn scar on the younger man's hand. So, we know he was the guy who attacked Marcus and tried to destroy the bones."

"But those bones weren't found anywhere near the mound, which seems to be the focus of the threat."

"What if he was scouting out the dig site to discover what we'd found and where we were working? Then he'd report back to the other man, the guy who followed me and the one you saw loitering by the van."

"Could be. And now you're digging into the mound they're getting serious about halting your work."

"Which isn't going to happen."

"Have you found anything else here?"

"I don't think I mentioned the leather pouch, which may be Victorian, and yesterday, Susan found a plastic buckle. They're all locked away at the house."

"Those items don't seem to be incriminating."

"I agree. And I told you about the few bones we located but from the deeper area. They're probably two to three hundred years old, and in my opinion, too far away from the artifacts to be connected."

"I wonder what the intruders are afraid of?"

"Something we haven't found yet." Grace hiked a shoulder. "Your guess is as good as mine."

"Except, they also threatened you."

"I told the students about our interesting evening, and all except Susan are adamant about staying. They feel obligated now to find what the bad guys don't want us to."

"Can you show me where Susan found the buckle?"

"Sure." She looped her arm through his and led him to the mound where the four students worked.

In his brief association with the crew, Logan had never seen Susan so focused. She carefully removed layer upon layer of dirt from a section.

"That's where she found the buckle." Grace pointed. "It might be nothing more than a trash dump site, items trodden underfoot and thus buried over time."

"But the intruders' threats last night indicate there's more to find."

"I know. That's why I want to stay." She coughed and then unwrapped a mint and popped it into her mouth.

"Hey, what's the matter?"

"Sore throat and the sniffles."

"Stress can compromise your immune system. You need to rest and drink plenty of fluids."

"Yes, Dr. Quinn, but I can't rest. I'm excited and want to be here for our next find."

He took her hand and walked toward the tent. "I can usually get my patients to cooperate by offering them stickers. Will that work with you?"

She giggled. "Nope. I'll need more than a little piece of paper to entice me to quit."

"Then I might have to resort to manhandling you." He lifted the flap and once inside the tent, he picked her up.

She threw her arms around his neck and surrendered to his kiss. "Mmm. That was nice, but I haven't changed my mind."

"Okay, but—" His phone buzzed. He set Grace down and checked the screen. "A text from Reggie. Mother is ranting about her grandfather and Nigel. I have to go."

"I understand. Let me know if I can do anything to help."

"Thanks." He kissed her again and before leaving the tent, turned. "I think it's time. I'll check Saturday or Sunday flights back to Texas. I'd love to stay here with you, but Mother needs a stable environment. You'd better be careful, young lady. I love you and don't want anything to happen to you while I'm gone."

CHAPTER 21

"Only one of the men has fingerprints on file. His name is Ivan Evans, and he lives in Great Rissington, not far from Bourton. So far, we haven't been able to locate him." Constable Lambert cleared her throat. "Please be careful and let us know if you see him again."

"Does he have a burn scar on his hand?" Grace switched the phone to her left ear.

"Yes. He has other scars on his torso, the result of an industrial accident years ago."

"He's the younger of the two intruders. Have you told Logan Quinn?"

"Yes. I just called him. We'll keep you posted." Lambert ended the call.

Grace closed her eyes. The rest Logan prescribed sounded great right now. She checked the time. Only two-thirty. She couldn't stay any longer. Shivering, achy, and congested, she phoned Peggy and with her permission, decided to go home. She stepped out of the tent and beckoned Marcus.

"What you need, prof? Hey, you don't look well."

"I'm not. Please take me home. The crew can work until dusk."

"Let's go." He caught Charles's attention. "I'm taking Dr. Gentry home. Be back in a few minutes."

Once at the house, she made herself a cup of hot tea and while waiting for it to brew, texted Logan.

You were right. I need rest. Going to bed. See you tomorrow.

Then she took a dose of decongestant meds, slid under the duvet on her bed, and fell asleep.

Out of the fog of medicated sleep, she checked the time. The crew should be home by now. She put in her hearing aids and sure enough, heard the students return and hoped they'd brought in whatever they'd found. She eased out of bed, threw on her warm robe over her clothes, and padded downstairs.

"Do you feel any better?" Kristy asked.

"A little but I'm so tired."

"Have you eaten anything?"

"Nope."

"I'll heat a bowl of soup for you. Why don't you have a nice hot bath and go back to bed?"

"Thanks. I will." The advice Kristy gave was spot on.

Grace slept until morning. She awoke less congested and with more energy. Dressed in layers against the damp cold, she descended the stairs and spied a tub on the dining room table. She checked the label marked with yesterday's date and the location in Tertius where the contents had been found.

Marcus entered the room, grinning. "Good to see you up. Have you looked in the tub yet?"

"No."

"I'll show you what we found." He pried open the lid and set it on a chair.

By now, the other students had joined them. Each watched with eyes wide and hands clasped in anticipation.

"Show me, then."

Marcus spread a cloth on the table. "Hey, Charles, please turn on the overhead light." Marcus lifted out two femurs and placed them on the special cloth. "We found almost a complete skeleton." He continued to arrange bones in an anatomical position.

Grace sat before her knees gave way. She couldn't believe her eyes. She squinted then blinked. "Wait. Wait. These bones were in the same area as the buckle?"

"Yes." Marcus picked up the skull and studied it. "I think…"

"Stop, everyone. Don't touch anything else. Did you find other artifacts, too?"

"We did." Kristy produced a plastic bag and set it on the table.

"What's in there?" A knot the size of Texas formed in Grace's gut.

"Degraded fabric from the same spot we found the buckle."

Grace rubbed her temples. Why had she left the students unsupervised?

Marcus sat beside her. "Did we do something wrong?"

"Unfortunately, yes. These bones are very new. As in less than twenty years old. Which makes the dig site—"

"A crime scene." Marcus leaned back. "I'm so sorry, Dr. Gentry. I should have paid closer attention. I…we got carried away."

"My fault, guys. Don't blame yourselves." Grace shook her head. The likelihood of excavating recent skeletal remains had not crossed her mind. Probably not Peggy's either.

"How were we supposed to know?" Susan sat and folded her arms.

"Well, two points. First," Kristy raised one finger. "The bones were found close to the artifacts which we know are not from the Anglo-Saxon period." She raised another finger. "Secondly, the lighter color of the bones should have been a clear indication."

"Yeah, but we had overcast skies all day, and toward evening, the light was fading. How could we notice bone color when we could hardly see our own feet?" Susan glanced at her peers.

"Stop." Grace scooted back her chair. "Kristy made valid points, but the fact remains, I shouldn't have left you unsupervised. Now, I need to call—" Her phone rang, the caller identified as Sir Barrette. "Good morning, Sir."

"I have a strange event I want to report. My farm manager noticed lights at the dig site late last night. When he investigated, he saw two men scampering over the area where you have the canopies. He chased them away and doesn't think they returned. Just thought I'd let you know."

"Thank you, Sir Barrette. We'll check it out right now." Grace repeated the news to the crew as she replaced the bones in the tub along with the plastic bag containing the fabric. "I'll call the police to report the find, and then, Marcus, please take me to the site. The rest of you stay here. I want one person in the house at all times."

"Okay, but I haven't had breakfast yet." Marcus picked up the tub and also snagged the van keys from the hook by the door.

"After you drop me off, you can get something. In fact, please bring me a coffee and a croissant." She ran upstairs and retrieved the bags containing the cameo, the comb, the leather pouch, and the plastic buckle. Dashing into the living room, she picked up her laptop and the camera. "Hey, guys, be prepared to make statements to the authorities, and we'll all need to provide DNA samples and have our fingerprints taken, for elimination purposes. See you later."

On the way to the site, Grace called Constable Lambert. She could tell by the panic in the policewoman's voice that she hadn't received such a call before.

"Will you be all right by yourself?" Marcus had stopped as close to the mound as he could drive.

"Yes. The authorities will be here soon. And look, that must be Sir Barrett's manager." She pointed to a middle-aged man dressed in a tweed jacket and waving at her. "I'll chat with him."

Grace received a firsthand account of what the man had seen the previous night. "I couldn't tell if they disturbed the site or not."

"Maybe you scared them off before they could. Thank you." She studied photographs of the area on the digital camera and then examined the hole where the skeletal remains had been located. "Please inform Sir Barrette we found new bones, as in this century. The police will be here soon, and they will cordon off the area."

"Oh, my. That's serious." He strode away toward the dense shrubbery.

Compared to the pictures, the area looked the same, but Marcus would have to verify her opinion. She checked inside the tent. Nothing had been disturbed in there. She sat and rubbed her arms. At least the shelter provided a respite from the biting wind.

When Marcus returned with coffee and pastries, he joined her in the tent. "I took a brief look around the mound. I don't think the intruders took anything."

"That's good news. Thanks for the breakfast. Please bring in the tub and then move our van to the parking area. This place will soon be swarming with police vehicles and a forensic team will set up their tents." The hot coffee soothed her tight throat. She should have asked Marcus for an extra-large cup.

Out of breath, he poked his head inside the tent. "I moved the van just in time and ran here to tell you two police cars have arrived."

Grace joined him as constables from one vehicle began to erect crime scene tape while Constable Lambert approached Grace and Marcus.

"I'll take your statements before a criminal investigator arrives."

Marcus described what the crew had found, ending with his excitement to show Grace that morning.

She explained why the team had removed the bones and accepted full responsibility. "We always take detailed photographs of any excavation, document each find in a logbook, and I know my crew was careful while handling the remains and the artifacts we've located."

"When the criminal investigator arrives, he'll want copies of the pictures. Where are the bones and items you found?"

"In the tent."

"I suggest you two wait in there until he comes. I'll check on my colleagues." Lambert said over her shoulder, "A reminder—no unauthorized people must enter the cordoned-off area."

Grace sat in the chair and drew her coat around her. She'd love another cup of coffee or tea.

"What's going to happen next?" Marcus paced between the table and the tent flap.

"The investigator will question us again. After that, he'll probably let us leave. Not much else will happen at the site until the forensic unit arrives."

The sound of tires on gravel alerted them to another vehicle. Lambert greeted the visitor. "This way, Detective Inspector."

In barged a tall, bald man about as rotund as any person Grace had seen. His jowls quivered when he spoke. "I'm DI James McDonald. I believe skeletal remains were removed from the site?"

Here we go again. Grace repeated the series of events that led to the present. Expecting a reprimand, she was surprised when he nodded and pointed to Marcus.

"You found the skeleton?"

"The crew and I did. Three other students who are at our residence in town."

"I know you have photographs, but come show me."

Grace picked up the camera and followed Marcus

and McDonald to the mound where Lambert raised the tape for them.

"Did you find anything there?" McDonald pointed to the deeper pit.

"Yes. A few human bones, probably two to three hundred years old." Grace noted the inspector paid little attention to the pit and stepped up to the shallower dig.

He smoothed his graying mustache. "And you would know."

"Yes. I—"

"That wasn't a question, Dr. Gentry. I know who you are and why you're here."

She shoved her cold hands into her pockets. "Then you understand why we weren't expecting to find a recent burial site."

"Yes, yes. Mr. Reid, show me exactly where you found the skeleton."

Grace frowned for a second. Mr. Reid? She seldom thought of her students' last names.

Careful not to disturb the area, Marcus indicated where the bones had been buried. "And over there on the other side of the wall, Susan found the piece of fabric."

McDonald turned to Grace. "Camera please." He examined the series of photographs. "Very detailed. Good. Forward them to me, please." He handed Grace a business card. "And now you both can leave. Lambert has your statements, and we know how to contact you." Walking off the mound, he pulled out his phone and made a call.

"We've been given our marching orders. Let's go." Marcus proceeded toward the parking area.

Grace hesitated, but accepting that her desire to be

a part of the investigation might be unrealistic, continued to their van where Marcus waited for her. Another white van approached with the characteristic yellow and blue markings of the UK police and Forensic Services in black letters on the side.

The driver stopped and his passenger climbed out and rounded the vehicle. "I thought I recognized you." She held out her hand. "Dr. Gentry, I've eagerly followed your work and am delighted to meet you. I'm Fiona Rushton, lead SOCO, Scene of Crime Officer for this investigation."

Stunned at the glowing compliment, Grace shook hands. "Pleased to meet you."

"Where are you going?"

"Home. We've spoken to DI McDonald, and he sent us away."

"Can you stay and help us? This *is* your area of expertise."

Did the sunshine just break through the clouds? Grace sure felt a surge of warmth infiltrate her body. "I'd love to, but I must check with my boss at Oxford first."

"Good. Hope to see you soon." Rushton returned to her van.

Grinning, Grace entered their vehicle and drew her phone from her pocket. She noted Logan had called and texted. A twinge of guilt nipped at her heels when she ignored him and hit Peggy's speed dial number.

Right now, she was Forensic Anthropologist, Dr. Grace Gentry.

CHAPTER 22

Another unanswered text. Grace must really be busy. Logan had spent most of the day ministering to Mother. Nothing major but she had constant demands on his time. She reminisced about his childhood, her college days, then back to her childhood. She refrained from mentioning Grandfather Gee, but she did talk a lot about her parents. Logan learned many interesting tidbits and wished he'd recorded her musings.

By mid-afternoon, Mother had worn herself out and went upstairs to nap.

Reggie had taken advantage of his presence and had gone shopping for items other than groceries. Home now, she deposited her purchases on the sofa, then asked, "Is Grace feeling better? Will she be coming for supper?"

"I don't know. She hasn't responded to my texts. I think I'll stop by the dig site."

"Okay. I'll make tea for Irene when she wakes. I can't wait to show her the dresses I bought."

Excitement bubbling up inside, Logan drove to the site. Talk about a hive of activity. Tents had multiplied. Vehicles were haphazardly parked everywhere as if dumped by a giant kid.

He slowed as he neared the parking area. White cars with yellow and blue markings. Police vehicles. Had the thugs returned and harmed Grace? He climbed out of the SUV and ran toward the hubbub.

A constable approached him. "You cannot enter this area."

"What's going on? Is…is someone hurt?"

"It's a crime scene, sir. Please return to your car."

Not ready to obey, he scanned the area. The crew's tent was in place, but their canopies over Tertius had been replaced by a blue and white tent. Crime scene tape cordoned off the whole mound, and—he just recalled—he didn't see Oxford's van in the parking lot. To pacify the constable, he stepped backward but had no intention of leaving yet. He texted Grace one more time. No response. If she and the crew weren't here, then they had to be at the house. Right. Back to the SUV but female voices caught his attention. Glancing over his shoulder at the new tent, he noted two people clad in white coveralls, masks, purple gloves on their hands, and blue booties on their feet.

One of them looked his way and raised a hand. "Hey, Logan. Don't go."

Grace. Finally

She negotiated the mound and walked toward him, stopped at the tape, and removed her mask. "I'm sorry I haven't communicated. As you can see ″

"I've been so worried about you." He reached out but dropped his hand. "I didn't know if you were sick, or seeing all this," he gestured to the police vehicles, "if the intruders had…had. Oh, my love, can I hug you?"

"Better not. We're investigating a crime scene."

"So I gather. But whew, I'm so thankful it's not the crime I imagined." His heart rose from his feet back to his chest. "I was worried."

"I'm sorry. I got so involved in the situation."

"What did you find?"

"Can't tell you. This is an ongoing investigation."

"Can you at least confirm that this is why the thugs threatened you?"

She pursed her lips but said nothing.

"So, yes. We should have paid them more attention. How long will you be working here?"

"I don't know. It all depends on what else we find."

"I take it you're working with the forensic team."

"I am." She grinned, eyes sparkling.

Her excitement did little to appease vestiges of his initial worry. "Don't overexert yourself. How are you feeling?"

"Good. The rest helped. What's happening in your world?"

He dug his heel into the soil. "I made our flight reservations for Sunday. No direct flights to Atlanta were available for Saturday. We'll leave the cottage Saturday afternoon and spend the night at a hotel close to Heathrow."

"So soon."

"Yes. Mother is fading fast, and I think we're both running out of steam."

Grace pointed toward the tent. "I need to get back to work. I'll find time tomorrow to say goodbye to

Irene and Reggie."

"I take it you haven't heard from UT."

"No." She tucked a strand of hair under her hood. "I'll let you know as soon as I do."

"Keep in mind that I love you, and I'll set up my practice wherever you find a job."

"I love you and I'll continue to pray for the UT position." She returned to the tent but before entering, she blew him a kiss.

He pretended to catch it and walked back to his SUV with his hand clutching an imaginary kiss.

CHAPTER 23

Bidding farewell to Grace was one of the most heart-wrenching things Logan had ever done. Seated beside her on the sofa while Mother and Reggie finished their breakfast in the kitchen, he wrapped his arms around her as tightly as possible. "We must Skype every day. I'll leave the time up to you."

Grace snuggled closer. "I will. Probably early evening."

"That'll be perfect."

"The students have returned to Oxford and will deliver all the ancient bones we found."

"So you walked here. I'll take you to the site when you're ready."

She moved away from him. "It's time." She hung

her head. "I'm going to miss you."

Cradling her face in his hands, he drew her to him and kissed her, at first, a tentative, gentle meeting of her soft, warm lips, then deeper and deeper until he had to breathe. "Whew. I'll keep the memory of that kiss in my heart." He stood and looked out at the garden, willing a tear to dry up before falling.

"I'll say goodbye to Irene and Reggie, then I must go to work." Grace entered the kitchen and hugged Irene. "I'm so glad you came to Bourton-on-the-Water."

"Me, too. Take care, my sweet child, and come see us in Texas."

"I will. Bye, Reggie." She grabbed her coat and was out the door before Logan had the car keys in hand.

"Are you staying warm in that forensic tent?" He opened her door.

"Yes. Those coveralls keep in body heat."

They didn't speak during the short drive up to the taped area.

"Call me this evening, please."

"I will. Bye, Logan." She leaned over and kissed him then hurried out of the SUV and up the mound.

He drove back to the cottage with a prayer on his lips. *Please, God, let her get the job in Austin. And keep us safe on our flight home.*

Packing his belongings took no time at all. He entered Mother's bedroom and noted all her clothes spread out on the bed. "Need some help?"

"Yes, but not from Reggie. She's too bossy."

Reggie stood in the hallway and shrugged. "I tried."

"Don't worry about it. Mother, where's your

suitcase?"

"I don't know."

Logan spied it on the other side of the bed. "Let's get started."

She was more interested in examining each item and commented on where she'd bought it or wore it. He folded her clothes and smiled. "Mother, fetch your toiletries from the bathroom."

"Okay, son."

He checked the wardrobe. Empty except for a few amber-colored capsules in the corner. He picked them up and frowned. They had to be Mother's, but he'd never seen them before. "Reggie, please come here a sec."

She walked in, carrying her suitcase. "I'm ready. What's the problem?"

Capsules in his open palm, he asked, "What are these?"

Clutching a cosmetic bag, Mother peered at them. "Those are mine. Reggie gives them to me. I must have dropped them."

"Well, Regina?"

She shrugged again. "Just some supplements that are supposed to help with…with anxiety."

"Have you given her anything else that I don't know about?" Anger simmering, he kept his tone neutral so as not to alarm Mother.

"No, only that one."

He studied her face. She looked him in the eyes and didn't blink. She seemed to be telling the truth. "No more, all right?"

Without another word, Reggie carried her suitcase from the room and went downstairs.

Truth or not, he had to quell his instinct to worry, and said, "Mother, please don't take any pills unless I give them to you. Okay?"

"Sure, son. Are we ready to leave?"

"Yes. Take your purse downstairs and collect your coat."

~~~

During the goodbye call to Grace, she prayed for their safe flight and for him to evaluate his relationship with God. He promised to do so. After they ended the call, he paced in his hotel room. He'd never told her why he was at odds with God and hadn't read anymore from the Bible. Although she hadn't pressed him, he knew she was sincere in her request for him to make changes. Since meeting Grace, he'd said a few simple prayers, but they were all asking for help. Now he dropped to his knees and bowed his head. "Father God, thank You for this avenue of communication. Thank You for Grace and her commitment to You and her love for me. Help me be a better person."

Ten minutes later, Tom Niven's son, Dennis, arrived at the hotel and drove them to Heathrow. Logan had never met the young man before, but they had a good chat about their UK visit.

"Please let your dad know how much we appreciate the use of the SUV. It certainly saved us a load of cash."

"No worries. He's giving it to me, so you saved me the cost of traveling to Edinburgh." Dennis stopped in the passenger unloading area. "I'll help get your luggage out of the boot."

Logan and Dennis shook hands, and then Mother waved as he drove away.
~~~

The trek through the airport to the ticket counter and then the gate exhausted Logan. No wonder Mother's steps slowed, and she kept asking for a cup of tea. They didn't have long to wait and were soon settled in their seats. Logan was overjoyed when he'd made the reservations because the airline didn't have three seats available together and Reggie was several rows back.

Soon after takeoff, lunch was served. Mother enjoyed the meal and then fell asleep.

Logan took out his laptop and reviewed notes recently received from his lawyer. Adrian was causing all kinds of ruckus in the press, and Logan needed to be prepared for the consequences. Several hours later, while Mother still slept, he squeezed down the aisle to the bathroom. On his way back he noted Reggie seated beside Mother. No need to panic. Maybe they were just chatting. But when he reached their row, he stopped and glared. Reggie had given Mother something and she was about to put it in her mouth. "Stop, Mother."

She looked at him and smiled. "It's all right, son. Reggie is my friend."

Logan reached over the woman and took the pills from Mother's hand. More capsules this time brown and orange. Before he lost his cool completely, he said through gritted teeth, "Leave, Reggie, before I throw you off the plane."

Reggie eased out of the seat. "No need to get angry. They're just vitamins."

"Sure, they are." Logan plopped into his seat, breathing as heavily as if he'd fought a gladiator. He turned to Mother hoping she'd give him a truthful answer. "Did you swallow any pills?"

She shook her head but then she shrugged. "I can't

remember. Oh, Logan, what's happening to me?"

He put his arms around her and patted her back like she'd done to him so many times during his childhood. "It'll be okay Mother. I'm here with you. Don't worry." But he was in that rocking chair Grace had mentioned, rocking away. What had Reggie been giving Mother? He'd have the capsules analyzed as soon as he was home. Vitamins—not likely. Had the supplements adversely affected her memory?

Checking through customs in Atlanta went smoothly, and then Logan sat with Mother while they waited for the connecting flight to Austin. Reggie kept her distance, for which Logan was thankful. He had no desire to communicate with her.

Mother sipped her iced tea and patted Logan's arm. "I want to talk to you about that young woman who came for dinner."

"Grace?"

"Yes. You love her, which is wonderful. Does she have a job in Texas yet?"

What was in the tea? Mother's recollection of parts of the conversations they'd had during those evenings was spot on. "She's waiting to hear from UT."

"And you? Where will you set up your new practice?"

No confusion. *Thank You, God.* "I'm not sure."

"Well, you must go wherever she gets a job. Tell me, what is it about her that made you fall in love so quickly?"

He drained his bottle of juice eager to respond. "She's um, unusual, dedicated, cares about others. Not to discount how cute she is and beautiful, but I instantly wanted to protect her, hold her close, and keep the world from hurting her." *All that and so much more.* "And she loves me. What more could a guy want?"

"That's great, son. She's the perfect match for you. Now, don't worry about me. I know I'll have to move out of my house soon. I've scattered brain cells all over England and don't have too many left. Just find me a place where I can have a little garden."

"I promise, Mother. But you'll be in your house for a long time yet." At first, the comment about brain cells amused him, then he turned to her.

She handed him her glass of tea and glanced up with a blank expression. "Why are we sitting in these uncomfortable chairs?"

And the lucid moments had vanished.

"We're waiting for our flight to Austin." The answer satisfied her, and she lay her head on his shoulder. Logan held her hand and continued to focus on her question about falling in love quickly. He and Grace were both in their mid-thirties, and this was not a first love for either of them. They were approaching this relationship from a place of maturity and experience. In the short time he'd known her, he'd come to believe they shared values and interests and mutual trust. He'd do anything for her, and he was certain she felt the same way. Sure, there was the physical attraction, but he'd never experienced such a deep emotional connection with a woman before.

The announcer called for their flight. He helped Mother stand and did a mental calculation. In less than a month, Grace would complete her assignment in Oxford. He had that much time to prove to himself and to her, that he was becoming a better man.

~~~
~~~

The next week crawled by for Logan. He'd moved into Mother's house and with her improved mental health, realized how much damage Reggie's capsules had caused. They'd been analyzed and were just over-the-counter supplements, but research indicated they adversely affected people with memory issues. The combination had almost proved deadly for Mother.

Reggie did stop by to collect her belongings. Logan cornered her, and asked, "Why did you give Mother a lethal combination of supplements?" He folded his arms and glared at her.

She sank into a chair at the kitchen table. "I know Irene has left me some money in her will—"

"This was all about money?" Logan clenched his jaw and his fists.

"Yes, sort of. I…my son's in trouble."

"Gambling debts?"

She nodded. "And I promised to help him."

"By causing Mother's early death?"

"No. I thought if her symptoms increased and in her confused state I could persuade her to give me my money now. She has so much, and she won't be needing…it…soon."

He thumped the table. "How dare you try to harm my mother? If this was all about money you could have asked for help. We would have given you some."

"I wasn't sure you would."

"You've ruined your chance of getting any now." He strode to the sink and turned. "I won't press charges if you go immediately and never contact Mother again. One more question. Did you tell Uncle Ken where we'd be in England?"

She lowered her head.

"Why? Oh, I see. You figured meeting Nigel would cause Mother anxiety and stress and add to her confusion." He pointed to the front door. "Please leave."

Reggie grabbed her suitcases and rolled them toward the foyer.

Watching the woman walk to her car, Logan shook his head and then closed the door. Mother could have asked Verna Yingling to accompany her. That friend, a retired nurse, offered, but Reggie won out. So sad that Mother's former friend allowed her son's problems to ruin their friendship.

With Reggie out of their lives, Logan had to find someone else to be a live-in companion. Verna lived in Austin and taking a chance she'd be available called and asked her to visit. Mother needed to provide input in the discussion, too. Although she seemed to improve day by day, the disease wasn't going away. While she was able to contribute to decisions, he wanted her involved. She still surprised Logan with the intelligent conversations she had with him.

During the evening's Skype with Grace, he told her all about Reggie's nefarious actions.

"I am so sorry Irene was subjected to her betrayal. I pray her symptoms will progress much more slowly, now."

"Thank you. Believe it or not, I have prayed for the same result."

"That's good to know."

She didn't press him on his relationship with God, for which he was grateful. Skype was not how he wanted to address the topic. "What's happening in Bourton?"

"We're all back in Oxford. I helped the SOCO team work the site for two days. We found no more skeletal remains. So only the remains of the male my team located were buried in the upper layer of the mound. We also found other jewelry, mostly costume, and of course bits of fabric, which may have been a backpack."

"The two intruders wanted you to stop digging so you wouldn't find that…man."

"Yeah. The younger man has been arrested. Ivan Evans. So far, he hasn't revealed the name of the other man, his boss."

"That is still good news." Logan explained his desire for Verna to stay with Mother so he could pack up his apartment in Cypress. "I'll look for something here, maybe with a six-month lease until…"

She beamed at him. "Until I know where I'll be working?"

"Right." Although they had declared their love for each other, he had not officially proposed yet and wasn't about to online. He decided then and there, he would return to England and propose before Grace left Oxford, providing Verna could stay with Mother.

"Why are you grinning?"

"I have a surprise for you. And that's all I'll say at the moment. Except I love you, miss you, and want you to be careful. The other bad guy is still out there."

"I think I'm safe in Oxford. I love you too. Please give my love to Irene."

"I will."

They ended the session and Logan hurried out of his room to find Mother.

She sat in the living room, watching TV. "Hey,

son. Come sit with me. What have you been doing?"

He'd explained the Skype process to her, but she still didn't quite understand. He told her anyway. "I've been chatting to Grace. She sends her love."

"In England?"

"Yep. And I have a question. Is your grandmother's jewelry in the safe?"

"Should be. Do you want it?"

"Only the engagement ring."

Although late in the afternoon, she was quick to make a connection. "For Grace?"

"Yes. If you don't mind."

"Why would I mind? I love that girl. Go get it."

Logan moved aside the painting of a still-life on the wall opposite, spun the dial, and entered the combination. He hoped Mother hadn't given the numbers to Reggie. Folders of papers and several jewelry boxes occupying the small shelves suggested she hadn't. He opened boxes until he found the exquisite ring, a ruby surrounded by diamonds. "When was your grandmother's birthday?"

"Oh, my goodness. Um…July something."

"The month is all I need. Thanks." A ruby was Grace's birthstone as she also had a July birthday.

His great-grandmother had been a small woman. The ring should fit Grace without any alterations. He returned the box to the safe and closed it. Now to make arrangements to fly back to England.

CHAPTER 24

Grace had been back in her flat in Oxford for almost a week. It was comforting to have the whole place to herself. Sipping coffee while she stared out the window at the ancient spires of college buildings, she decided to take a break from writing reports and setting assignments for her students. After the church service that morning, she'd go exploring. Her stint in Oxford was fast drawing to a close and she probably wouldn't return any time soon.

Dressed warmly for her excursion, she caught the bus to church. As usual, she prayed for Logan and Irene, and her next job. Returning to the USA was both exciting and frightening. If she wasn't offered the job at UT, she'd have to reevaluate her choices. Hold out for a professorship at a university, or teach high school classes? Or… just be a wife and hopefully a mother. But Logan had yet to propose. Could she presume he would? She knew he wouldn't suggest they live together, which she wouldn't agree to anyway and she was old-fashioned enough to want him to ask her to marry him. What about his relationship with God? He was a good person as demonstrated by his love for and care of Irene. Was that enough? Could she be happy with a man who didn't share her faith?

The service concluded with the singing of one of her favorite old hymns "The Lord's My Shepheard". Grace chatted with a few people and then set off on her adventure. During her time in Oxford, she'd explored many areas, especially the numerous colleges that were part of the university. The architecture of the buildings was fascinating, especially the older ones. The Merton College Chapel dated back to the thirteenth century. However, today she decided to explore the Christ Church Meadow, a vast scenic park with the college buildings forming one boundary. She planned to complete the two-mile walk then get a bite to eat and return to her flat.

The tree-lined avenue drew her like a magnet. She ambled down Poplar Walk relishing the crunch of fall-colored leaves underfoot. So much beauty surrounded by centuries of academic learning. Few people enjoyed the park that morning which was all right with her. About an hour into her trek, the walk turned north to follow the River Cherwell. Chirping birds and the gentle ripple of water serenaded her.

She drew in a satisfying breath and then a strong arm circled her waist from behind while another caught her in a headlock. Surprise and fear stifled her voice. She tried to scream but no sound emerged.

Struggling only tightened the man's hold. He drew her closer to a clump of bushes along the river. Two women jogged past, and he slackened his grip. Grace scratched the hand at her waist and bent her knees. He loosened the arm around her neck. She ran. But he was on her heels and grabbed her arm. She swung around. If he was going to harm her, she wanted to know who he was. She recognized the older intruder, the one who held a knife to Irene's throat. His offensive body odor should have been enough reminder.

"Why are you doing this?"

He held a hand over her mouth. "Be quiet."

Shaking her head, she glared at him. He moved his hand a smidge and she mumbled through his finger, "We found the body. And some jewelry. That's why you threatened me, isn't it? Why assault me now? The cops are after you."

"I know. My brother has been arrested and I'm on the run. My life is over."

"Like the man we found? His life is over. Did you kill him?"

"No comment." He spun her around, but before he could encircle her waist with his arm again, she lifted her foot as hard as she could and caught him in the groin. He let go, and she ran. He grabbed her coat and pulled, stopping her escape. She lashed out at him but was no match for his superior size and strength. However, she wasn't going quietly. She wriggled and squirmed and screamed for help. He stumbled and lost his footing.

The next thing she knew, she was in the cold water with him on top of her. He held her down in the shallows. She flayed her arms and kicked out, to no avail. Although holding her breath longer than she'd ever had to before, she felt the rocks digging into her back. She curled her fingers around one and swung it toward him. It caught him on the temple. He released her. She gasped for air and tried to get up, but he seized one leg. Underwater again, she grabbed another rock. This time the force of her blow sent him into the water, too.

She heard a muffled shout. Strong arms pulled her up. She panted for air while splashing through the river to solid ground. Out of the corner of her eye, she noticed the mugger flee.

Hours later, after being treated at A & E, England's version of the ER, and being questioned by the police, she took a taxi home. She suffered bruising, lost one hearing aid, the other one water-damaged beyond repair, and her phone ruined. All problems in their own right, but her shattered self-confidence was her main concern. Never had she felt so vulnerable. She longed for Logan's powerful arms and broad chest and comforting presence.

She and Logan had Skyped every evening. Could she face him tonight, bruised face and all? Yes. Keeping secrets was not a good idea in a new relationship. She texted him and suggested they chat earlier than usual. Their mid-afternoon calls were fine for him in Texas, and with the time change, ten o'clock meetings suited her well. However, that evening as exhausted as she was, she'd fall asleep during the session.

Laptop ready at eight, Grace sat on her bed surrounded by fluffy pillows. Her old hearing aids were good enough until she could replace them in Texas, but in the morning, she'd purchase a new phone. She had her bedside lamp on, hoping the muted light would minimize the bruises and scrapes on the side of her face. After she gave a brief description of her experience, Logan had the response she expected. At first, he was outraged, but then he offered sympathy and support.

"What did the police say?"

"I told them about the events in Bourton and gave them Lambert's and McDonald's names. I also told them this man's brother had already been arrested. Now we wait."

"You must be careful. This guy is free to attack you again."

"I don't think he will. He wanted someone to blame for his misdeeds. He knows the cops are after him."

"I'll pay for a bodyguard." His tone dripped with anxiety.

"No need, but thanks. Usually, I'm surrounded by crowds of people."

"But I want you to be safe." He glanced to the side then back at the screen. "Do you have much to pack up before you leave England?"

"No. My flat is furnished, so I just have my personal items. I haven't purchased much since being here. Too busy with the assignment and sight-seeing."

"You know, if Mother was healthy, I'd be over there in a shot." He moved closer to the computer. "I miss you. Every hour of every day."

Heat infused her cheeks. "I miss you, too." Now was the perfect time. "I have some good news."

"Please share. I don't want to leave you thinking about the attack and your beautiful but bruised face."

"I was very busy yesterday and only checked the post when I returned from the hospital this afternoon." She waited a second to add the punch line.

He raised his eyebrows. "And?"

"A letter from UT." She clasped her hands and grinned. "I got the job."

"Woohoo!" He jumped up, almost knocking his laptop off the desk. "That is fantastic. When do you start?"

"Mid-January."

"I'm so happy I can hardly think. What should I do first?" He rubbed his chin. "Call Dana and ask if she still wants me to join her practice. And, and…"

How about asking me to marry you? "I need to find a place to live." Would that prompt him?

"Don't worry about that. You can stay with Mother for a while. She has a four-bedroom house. And you can use her car if need be."

Not the response she desired. She yawned and hid a smile. At least he'd be close to Irene and that enhanced her happiness.

After ending the session, she slid under the covers. She might have to go against her rule and propose to him if he didn't act soon.

CHAPTER 25

Plans to return to England were put on hold until Logan arranged for a live-in companion for Mother. Her friend, Verna, had visited, and although she agreed to consider the proposal, hadn't responded yet.

In the meantime, he contacted his son and asked if he would fly to Austin for Thanksgiving the following week.

At first, their conversation was strained, and Logan couldn't blame Corey for that. "I know I haven't been in your life much, but I want to change that."

"A bit late. I consider Frank my dad."

Corey's comment regarding his stepfather struck Logan's heart, but he deserved the jab. "I know, and I understand. Would you consider coming for your grandmother's sake?"

"That's low, even for you…Dad."

"She asks after you, and you know, she isn't well."

"How long do I have to stay? I don't want to mess up my week off school."

Ouch. Another jab. "Two, three days."

"I'll think about it."

And with that comment, Logan had to be satisfied. He wouldn't tell Mother until the flight arrangements had been made.

He had one more contact to make that also might not conclude in his favor. Dana Booth had suggested he join her pediatric practice in Round Rock, but he wondered if her offer had been made in sympathy. To find out, he had to ask. Chickening out of speaking to her in person, he emailed.

Verna had not made a decision yet, and Logan needed to pack up his apartment in Cypress and arrange storage for his furniture. He remembered Grace had said she sold up before accepting the assignment in England. To begin their lives together, they could use his furniture. It wasn't fancy, but he didn't think she was the type of person who splurged on material items.

He could hire a day nurse but asked Mother first. "I need to drive to Cypress to close up my apartment."

Her eyes sparkled.

"Would you like to come with me? It's a two-and-a-half-hour drive."

She scooted her chair back from the kitchen table and hugged him. "I'm ready to travel with my favorite son, but only if we can stop in Brenham for ice cream."

Not a problem. They agreed to leave early the next morning. Not only was Mother looking better, but she also had more energy and recalled many details from her past. Such as Brenham being home to the Blue Bell ice cream factory. When friends visited her from out of state, she'd always made a point of taking them there. Sure, she could purchase the ice cream at most grocery stores, but she insisted the treat tasted better in

Brenham, especially if they toured the factory.

That evening, Logan explained his plans to Grace. "I'm so glad she's excited about the trip. We can stop often along the way, spend the night, and return the next day."

"It sounds like fun. I pray for her mental acuity daily."

"Would you believe, so do I?"

She gave him a sweet smile. "That news cheers me, too." The bruises on her face had changed color.

"How are you? Any ill effects from your dreadful experience yesterday?"

"Achy and more bruises are evident. My students are very considerate. Even Susan."

He wanted to tell her his plan to return to England, but he'd have to wait until Mother had a companion who wouldn't sabotage her health.

The next morning, he helped Mother pack an overnight bag, and then they set out for Cypress. No matter the time of day, traffic heading to or from Houston was always heavy. He made the prerequisite stop in Brenham for ice cream, but they didn't tour the facility. Later, after he'd packed his clothes and a few other items he wanted, Mother accompanied him to the apartment manager's office. Logan had one month left on his lease. He paid the rent and provided the moving company's details.

Cypress had been a good place to live and work, but he wouldn't be sorry to see the last of it. His phone buzzed with a text. Wayne Hammond insisted they talk immediately. He deposited two large suitcases and assorted tote bags into the back of his SUV, helped Mother into the passenger seat, and then dialed

Wayne's number. "What's the urgency?"

"You are not going to believe what Adrian Kerns has done. Not only is he appealing his sentence, but he also says you paid the nursing staff to lie."

Logan stepped away from his vehicle. "What?"

"You heard me. We need to meet."

"I'm in Cypress. Just packed up my apartment."

"Well, get yourself back to Austin ASAP."

"Okay."

He canceled the hotel reservations, and Mother had no objection to the drive. Her only request was he play soothing music for her.

Back in Round Rock, she retreated to her room to nap, and Logan called Wayne again. "I'm home. You'll have to come here as I can't leave Mother alone."

~~~

Reassured by Wayne that Adrian's accusation probably wouldn't go far as he had made no mention of the payment during his trial. However, he declared Logan had threatened his life if he did discuss it. This latest allegation would only destroy whatever fragments remained of Logan's reputation.

He did receive one bright spot of news. Verna accepted the position and agreed to move in the following day. With Mother's needs taken care of and with the assurance from Wayne that he could leave the country, Logan booked his ticket to England. He had to accept an economy seat and dreaded the long flight with his knees under his chin. But, to see Grace, he'd ride in the baggage compartment if necessary.

During the Skype session that evening, Logan had a hard time keeping his secret. He bombarded Grace with questions so she wouldn't toss any his way. Her
~~~

bruises and scrapes were healing, but before she said goodbye, she frowned and didn't appear to be as content as in their previous chat.

Having Verna in the house was like the proverbial breath of fresh air. She made Mother laugh reminiscing about events from their years of friendship. She informed Logan the reason she hadn't immediately accepted the job had nothing to do with Irene, but she had to make arrangements for other members of her church to serve in their soup kitchen.

With Mother's needs taken care of, Logan was able to meet with Wayne and provided information he could use to counter Adrian's accusation. Wayne suggested he handle it all and for Logan to stay as far away as possible.

Grace had good news to share during their next Skype session. "Ivan Evans has finally blabbed in jail. He gave the police possible places where his brother might be hiding, and also alluded to more bodies Martin buried. He said he wasn't sure of an exact location because he wasn't involved as he had been burying the body by the lakes in Bourton. However, the police don't believe him."

"I'm glad he talked, but I won't be satisfied until the brother is apprehended, too. You have to come home to me all in one piece."

"I'll be careful."

Toward bedtime, Mother cornered Logan in the living room. "Hey, son. I'm glad Verna is here, but what happened to Reggie?"

He didn't want to lie, but he wasn't sure she could handle the whole truth. "Reggie gave you pills that weren't prescribed and were making you more forgetful."

"Why? That doesn't sound like something a friend would do."

How true. "She wanted, um, you to get sick and…" Nope. He couldn't complete the thought. "She wanted money."

"All she had to do was ask."

Logan took Mother's and. "I know, sweet lady. Let me help you to your room." At some point, he needed to talk with her about changing her will.

His flight to Atlanta left early the next morning. He'd already provided Verna with all the meds, money, and contact details she'd need while he was gone, and remembered to get the ring from the safe. He only intended to stay four days, long enough to propose and be back home for the week of Thanksgiving in case Corey wanted to visit longer.

There'd be no need to Skype that evening. He'd be able to hold Grace and chat with her all night.

CHAPTER 26

As part of the conclusion to the students' excavation experience in Bourton-on-the-Water, Grace informed them about her work with SOCO.

"That's what I want to do," Kristy said.

"You'll be an asset to the program. You're a quick learner and pay close attention to detail."

Head lowered, Susan muttered something. The almost permanent pout marred her face.

"Sorry, Susan. I didn't hear you. I'm wearing old aides that aren't as sensitive."

"I said, what about me?"

"You need to develop confidence in your skills." Grace wanted to add she shouldn't rely on tearing someone else down to boost her self-esteem. "With time, you'll become a competent anthropologist."

"I'd rather work with ancient skeletal remains." Charles leaned back in his chair. "I don't want to focus on recent crimes."

"If you gain satisfaction from what you do, then your daily work is not a chore." Grace understood the concept all too well. Although she'd enjoyed the visiting professorship, she would be happy to spend a lot of her time doing research.

After she'd received the letter of appointment, she checked the Texas Archeological Research Lab online. Located on UT's North Campus, the facility was only ten miles or so from Round Rock. What could be more perfect? *A proposal maybe.*

Seated close to Grace, Marcus crossed his arms. "I'm not sure what I'd prefer. Working in Bourton was very rewarding, but it would have been more so if the site hadn't been excavated previously. If we were the first on the scene."

"You only have two weeks left in the term. I want you to complete the chronicling of your experiences in Bourton. Be sure to include the pros and cons of working at the site. And I have a list of the last readings I require." She checked her watch. "That's all for today. See you tomorrow."

But the meeting the next day wouldn't happen. Peggy entered Grace's office, closed the door, and shook her head.

"What's the matter?" Muscles knotted in Grace's stomach. Her boss did not look happy.

"I received a request from the SOCO team you worked with in Bourton. They want you to return to the village to help with another recent burial site."

"Will you approve the request?"

"I will, reluctantly."

"When do they want me there?"

"Now, or at least tomorrow."

Nothing she'd like more. Her knotted muscles relaxed. "The local police notified me the man they arrested admitted his brother may have buried more bodies."

"I see. Well, I know you'll do us proud."

"Can I take my students with me? This experience would be beneficial."

"No. They've had all the field experience they need for now." Peggy spun around and left the office.

Grace hurried home and packed a suitcase. She wanted to be in Bourton ready to work first thing in the morning. Fiona Rushton, the lead SOCO she'd met previously, agreed to meet the late rain in Moreton-in-Marsh.

Although she always looked forward to their nightly Skype sessions, Grace was glad Logan had texted he wouldn't be able to see her that evening. She didn't want him to worry about her working at another burial site connected to Martin Evans.

Once settled in her hotel room in Bourton, Grace texted Logan.

Our Skype meeting tomorrow night should be quite exciting.

~~~

Fiona and her team had already marked out the areas to be excavated. Ivan had finally given the cops more information. He indicated a place along Rissignton Road, east of Bourton. Thick trees and brush covered a wide expanse parallel to the road, which made the process more difficult. Cadaver search dogs had identified two possible burial sites, close together. The sparse vegetation added to the certainty of recent remains being there, human or animal. A large blue and
~~~

white tent shielded the area.

"Do you have any idea when these people were buried here?" Grace slipped on the purple nitrile gloves.

"The informant suggested at least three years ago. He said as far as he knew, there are only two bodies." Fiona handed Grace a bucket containing the necessary tools. Brushes of various sizes, a hand shovel, a large trowel and a smaller one. "I'm so glad you're with us. Let's begin." She knelt at one corner of the first site and pointed to another marked area two meters away. "I'd like you to work over there, please."

Grace shoved aside all personal thoughts and problems and took a breath. This was such an important job. Locating the remains of a missing person could provide family members or loved ones with— The word that popped into her head was "closure" but she hated it. Closure to what? Grief, the feeling of emptiness? She preferred finality. They could finally stop the search, or end the worry about what might be happening. Hold a funeral and say goodbye.

She'd removed about eighteen inches of dirt and used the shovel to cut through a few roots, but the change in soil color indicated she was in the right area. Further into the hole, the trowel scraped against something solid. Grace leaned over and brushed dirt off the object. Yes. The top of a cranium. "Found a skull." Strands of dark brown hair clung to the parietal bone. She took her time to remove the dirt without damaging the hair.

Another tech took photographs as Grace continued exposing the skeletal remains of a child. Steeling herself against the raw emotion threatening to cripple her, she worked without a break until the complete skeleton lay before her. The presence of ligaments, tendons, and some soft tissue indicated the child was buried two and a half to three years ago and might have been six or seven years old. The time frame fit with the details Ivan provided. Remnants of clothing clung to some bones, and bits of shoes still encased the feet.

Fiona had also located a child's remains. "Hey, Grace. Come see what else I found buried beneath the body."

Careful not to knock dirt back into the hole, Grace rose and stepped to the other site.

"Look, a bag." Fiona held up a navy-blue rectangular bag, probably made from a synthetic fabric, as it was still in good condition.

"Is there anything in it?"

"No. Too bad, because I think it's a child's school bookbag. If it contained books, we'd be able to use them to identify the victims."

"How old do you think your child was?" Grace forced the emotion from her voice.

"Between five and seven."

"Mine, too." She backstepped to her site. "Since your child had a school bag, I'll keep working to see if my child did, too." The similarities were not lost on Grace. Two children here in a recent burial, and the two children they'd found in Tertius, buried hundreds of years ago.

"Good idea. I'll inform the Gloucestershire Constabulary about our find."

Grace dug deeper but found no artifact. She widened her search area and uncovered the strap of a bag to the left of where the body had been buried. Slow and deliberate removal of dirt and she uncovered the school bag, also navy blue. However, this one contained a small doll and a hairbrush.

Resting on her haunches, she placed the items in plastic bags, then sealed them and completed the identification information. The dark brown hair in the brush appeared to match what was still attached to the skull. The remains provided several sources from which to extract DNA. A family somewhere would soon be able to claim their child. Fiona had explained the police were searching Missing Person databases for disappearances about three years ago. Any information she and Grace provided would hasten the process.

She turned and looked at Fiona. "Here's an idea. What if these two are siblings? Their hair is the same color and their bookbags match. They could have attended the same school."

"Possible. However, many schools use navy blue bags." Fiona picked up her tools. "Once I've uncovered skeletal remains, I don't speculate about them and their families or their lives before the tragedy. Are you ready to close up shop?"

Not the response Grace expected. True, she usually spent too much time wondering about the lives the victims led before they died. Shrugging, she returned to her site to collect the tools. Light from the high-powered lamp in the corner glinted off a white speck in the hole. She knelt and brushed away the dirt around the object. It couldn't be. She brushed away more dirt and exposed a small bone. The child's skeleton had been complete. There might be another body buried here. Holding the bone between thumb and forefinger, she gave it a thorough visual examination. She was correct. A human carpal. An adult-sized bone.

"Fiona, come here, please. We have a problem." She held out the bone to her colleague.

"Are you joking? Where'd you find it?"

"Under the child's skeleton. There." Grace pointed to the area she'd excavated.

"Seriously?"

She nodded.

"Well, I suppose we're not done." Fiona pursed her lips, stepped closer to the site where Grace worked, and began scraping at the dirt about a meter from her. "This isn't the first time an informant lied."

Minutes later, Grace uncovered more adult bones, some broken, and none in anatomical order. "This skeleton has been disturbed after burial. The bones are widely scattered."

Fiona sat on the rim of the hole and lifted out a bone, a femur. "Probably male by the length of the bone."

"These remains have been here longer than the children. They are a shade darker, and I haven't found any clothing yet. Have you?"

"Maybe…" Fiona brushed away more dirt. "Yes, it's a leather belt."

"Leather deteriorates much slower than other materials. We can't age the burial site by the belt."

Fiona stopped digging and looked at Grace. "Even in this light and without the child's bones as a comparison, you could tell these are a different color?"

"Yes. Only a shade darker and so far none have tendons or ligaments present. A couple have faint scrapes as if damaged by a shovel."

Her colleague studied the femur. "I would have noticed the marks when I examined them back at the lab."

They worked side-by-side for another hour, each finding various bones and scraps of fabric. Grace had uncovered a femur and noted a healed break, a detail to help identify the remains.

At about the same time, Fiona announced. "Another femur."

"Wait a minute. I just found one, too." She rolled her stiff shoulders. "That means we have two bodies here."

"Our informant omitted a lot from his statement about his brother."

Now, Grace knew for certain who had buried the bodies—Martin Evans.

During an afternoon tea break, she checked her messages. A text from Logan intrigued her.

You say our Skype session tonight will be interesting. I think it will be surprising!

What could he mean? He'd secured a place in a new practice? He'd rented a grand apartment? She'd have to wait several hours to find out.

CHAPTER 27

The train from Heathrow Airport to Oxford had been delayed and Logan arrived mid-afternoon. While he walked to the university, he used his phone to provide the address for the School of Archeology. Thirty minutes later, he approached the building and recognized a man walking toward him. Marcus. A great coincidence.

"Logan? What are you doing here? I thought you were back in America."

"I was, but I'm looking for Grace."

"She's not here."

"As in the building or the city?" His heart rate increased.

"She was called back to Bourton."

"Why?" Marcus's response did little to calm Logan's heart.

"Dr. Wilson said she's helping at another burial site and will be there a few days." Marcus turned up the collar of his jacket against the brisk wind. "That's all I know. I have to go, Logan." He hurried down the sidewalk.

Another burial site connected to Martin Evans? Logan hitched the strap of his duffle bag higher on his shoulder. Only one way to find out. He needed transportation to Bourton-on-the-Water. He could catch a train but decided to rent a car so he'd have the use of a vehicle in the village.

Halfway to his final destination, he realized he didn't ask Marcus where Grace was working or staying. He could text her, but that would spoil the surprise. There probably wouldn't be more than one location where Forensic Services tents were erected. He'd ask folks in the village or drive around and only contact Grace as a last resort.

The possibility the burial site was associated with Martin Evans filled him with dread. He swallowed against the boulder in his throat. The man had yet to be arrested, and he'd attacked Grace in Oxford. Would she be safe back in Bourton? Logan made the trip in under an hour. Although slanted rays from the weak sun glistened off the colorful trees, dusk fast approached. He stopped at various cafés, shops, and hotels, but no one knew the location of the site.

Standing outside the Post Office, he looked up and down the High Street. A police car passed him and continued east toward Birdland. Logan ran to his car but jerked to a stop. A man wearing a familiar windbreaker loped down the sidewalk outside the grocery store. Martin, the thug who had threatened Mother and attacked Grace wore such a coat. Logan gave chase. However, the man heard him and darted up a side street. By the time Logan reached the corner, Martin had disappeared.

He dialed the number he'd been given for the area police station and reported the sighting. Constable Lambert assured him they'd follow up. He asked her where SOCOs were working, but she wouldn't tell him. No problem. He called Grace and left a message about seeing Martin, then hurried back to his vehicle and drove in the same direction the police car had. About half a mile later, he spotted the car parked on a side street behind a civilian sedan and a Forensic Investigation Unit's van. Thick vegetation covered the land to his left. He slowed and pulled onto the narrow shoulder. There was no official activity on the other side of the road designated as Home Farm and surrounded by a wall.

Maybe a police officer was in the car. Logan approached the vehicle and then noticed crime scene tape cordoning off a large area among the trees and shrubs, and a blue and white tent in the distance. He knew not to cross the tape and stood beside the empty car, hoping to catch someone's attention. All his calls to Grace went straight to message. The techs had erected floodlights, no doubt expecting to work late.

Since he knew where Grace worked and that police officers were present, he drove back to the village and reserved a hotel room. When he returned to the site, the police car was gone. He parked along Rissington Road again, this time across from the side street so he could see the techs when they emerged. One man and two women stopped at the van and removed their protective coveralls. He was about to call out to them when another, shorter person emerged from the brush. She removed her hood, and the wind tousled her black ponytail. Grace.

Pointing back the way she came, she lifted the tape. Big mistake. Arms clad in black grabbed her. The assailant must have covered her mouth because she didn't scream. Logan ran across the road, alerted the other SOCOs to Grace's predicament, and dashed under the tape. The vegetation wasn't as dense as it appeared from the road. He followed the sound of twigs snapping, zigzagging away from the dig site still illuminated by the floodlights. Deeper and deeper he went until he heard nothing but the occasional twittering bird.

He stopped and scanned the area. Grace's white coveralls should be easy to spot, but he didn't see her. His racing heart sent blood thumping in his ears. He risked turning on his phone's flashlight and shone it around. Trees, shrubs, and an open field to his left, but no humans. Then a faint whimper. He turned off the light to prevent the man from knowing his location, but try as he might, he couldn't forge ahead quietly. Why not take advantage of the situation? He barged through the brush, adding his voice to the commotion. "I know where you are, Martin." Making the assumption added conviction to his threat. "You'd better let her go. If you hurt her—"

A low growl and a high-pitched scream. Logan shone his light again and the beam landed right in the thug's eyes.

Martin shook his hand and squealed, "She bit me."

"That's the least of your worries." Noticing Grace at a safe distance, Logan pounced on him. Martin was no match for his anger-fueled strength and didn't even dodge when Logan aimed a fist at his chin. Ready to inflict another blow, he grabbed the man's collar, but

Grace intervened.

"I'm fine, Logan. Please, don't hit him again."

By now, another SOCO arrived on the scene. "We called the police. I'll lock the man in the van until they arrest him." The burly tech twisted Martin's arm behind his back, flicked on a flashlight, and led him away.

Logan drew Grace to him. "Are you sure he didn't hurt you?"

She nodded against this chest. "What are you doing here?"

He chuckled. "This is not the surprise I had in mind."

"No matter why you're here, I'm thankful you are."

Shining his light, he led the way back to the van. "I missed you so much. Are you finished with the site?"

"No. We'll be back tomorrow. We found complete remains of two young children, but underneath one body, we located bones of at least two adults." Grace stepped out of her coveralls and dumped all her protective gear beside the van. She introduced Logan to her colleagues.

"Good thing you noticed that man take Grace. None of us was paying attention." Fiona patted Grace's shoulder. "Glad you're okay."

Sirens announced the arrival of the police. Constable Lambert arrested Martin and placed him in the back of her squad car.

"See if he will tell you how many bodies he buried here." Grace nodded to Lambert. "We found two children in one area and bones of at least two adults in a deeper grave. Finally, both men who threatened Irene and me are in custody." She collected her purse and coat from Fiona's car. "Logan can bring me in the morning. Good night."

Logan set his arm around her shoulders and guided her across the street to his car. "Thank you for stopping me from hitting Martin again. I was so angry, I wanted to…" Ashamed of what he might have done, he hung his head.

"I understand. If given the opportunity, I would have hit him. It's amazing what protective instincts kick in when a loved one is in danger."

"I wish you could come back home now instead of waiting until the term is over."

"Excavating the rest of the bones here will be my culminating work in England. I'll feel vindicated after finding out who these people were that Martin killed. He seemed to be the mastermind, and Ivan his poor brother his stooge."

"Do you think you'll be working here on Sunday?" He opened the passenger door for her.

"I don't know. With both of us concentrating on one area, we might find all the bones and artifacts. Tomorrow."

Logan started the car and turned up the heat. "My return ticket is for Tuesday. I'd like some time to talk before then, just the two of us."

"I'll make time." Although Grace smiled at him, she had dark circles under her eyes and looked as if she'd fall asleep any minute.

"Can we at least have supper together tonight?"

"Of course. The pub in my hotel serves great food."

"It's a date then."

Wrapping her arms around herself, she asked,

"What will you do tomorrow?"

"That, my dear love, is a surprise." His turn to smile. He planned on finding out how he and Grace could marry before he returned to Texas.

CHAPTER 28

Her wrist alarm clock shocked her awake. Used to the mild zap, Grace rubbed her eyes and climbed out of bed. She'd enjoyed the evening meal with Logan and appreciated the fact he recognized her exhaustion and said good night at her hotel room door. They'd arranged to meet for a quick breakfast before he took her to the dig site.

He rose from an armchair as soon as she entered the lobby. "Morning, my love. Sleep well?"

"Yup. Knowing you're in town and the two thugs are in jail, brought me some peace of mind."

"Something else bothering you?"

They chose a booth, and he slid in beside her. She ordered coffee and an omelet and he did the same.

Holding her hand, he asked again, "Are you all right?"

His large hand engulfed hers in a warm embrace. "I want to know who the children are." She looked at him. "And the adults, but it's the children who are on my heart."

He kissed her forehead. "I understand."

The soft expression covering his face matched his words. He did understand her need for the children to be identified.

During the meal, she asked about Irene.

"She is so much more alert now Reggie is no longer administering the supplements that added to her confusion. Verna, her friend, is a great asset. Mother enjoys her company and was more than happy for me to come see you."

"Good. I'm happy she's doing well. Any news about your future practice?"

"Not yet. Dana knows I'm here with you. She asked to meet—which is a good sign. I'll make arrangements when I return."

Logan drove Grace to the site and waited with her until Fiona arrived. "Have you changed your mind about telling me your plans for the day?"

"Nope." He grinned. "Text me when you're ready to leave. Can I bring you lunch?"

"Thanks, but no. Fiona has made arrangements." She leaned over and became lost in his kiss. Whew, that man's kisses could set her blood on fire.

Dressed in coveralls and other protective gear, she followed Fiona to the tent. Although the Evans brothers were in custody, there'd been an overnight guard at the site. SOCOs had made the assumption the adult bodies were also buried by Martin, but they were taking no chances.

Hour after hour, Grace worked locating more bones of three adults as another femur indicated. She and Fiona widened the search with the newly exposed area corresponding to where the other child had been found.

Considering the artifacts unearthed, the adults had been buried about three years before the children. Martin—if he were responsible for the burial—had been meticulous in not including any identifying objects such as wallets. However, he'd not searched the men's clothing well enough. Grace found a scrap of denim which appeared to be part of a pocket that contained a fragment of a ticket. Under a microscope, she determined the concert ticket was dated May 2017. The find was a highlight of her morning's work. Now the authorities had an end date to use in searching the Missing Person database.

During a lunch break, Fiona received a text. The children had been tentatively identified as twins who were abducted on their way to school in Gloucester three years ago. Their parents had paid the ransom, but the children were never returned.

On hearing the news, tears welled up in Grace's eyes. After DNA confirmation, the parents might find a measure of peace knowing their children were not suffering. She walked back to the tent recognizing a twinge of sadness still tugged at her heart because she'd found a child's remains. But this time the discovery was less devastating. She had Logan in her life, a possible future with him, and maybe a family of their own.

The excavation continued into the afternoon. Grace found more bones, many in anatomical position, indicating they had not been disturbed when Martin dug the child's grave. The locating of a skull with the mandible and maxilla intact meant the teeth could be used for identification. "Look, Fiona." Grace pointed to line fractures radiating from a jagged hole in the parietal bone. "Looks as if this chap suffered a nasty blow to the head." Tufts of light-colored hair surrounded the hole.

Fiona had also found bones which appeared to have been undisturbed. "Same here." She held up a skull with the left temporal bone shattered. "Possible causes of death. Poor guys."

By dusk, Grace had located most of the bones of the third man. He'd been shot, with the bullet still lodged in his first lumbar vertebra. His skull still wore the remnants of a dark brown toupee made from nylon strands which resembled real hair remarkably well. Maybe another means of identification.

Along with the skeletal remains, she and Fiona had found scraps of clothing, especially denim which appeared to have a synthetic component in the fabric, bits of canvas and plastic grommets probably from trainers.

Close to six o'clock, Fiona called a halt to the excavation. "We've been digging for thirty minutes without finding any more bones or artifacts. Each body is missing a few tarsals and carpals and related small bones. One has five broken ribs and some of the pieces are missing, but I conclude we've found all we're going to of these bodies. Do you concur, Dr. Gentry?"

"I do. In my opinion, the few bones we haven't located would not aid in determining the causes of death or provide additional means of identification. The artifacts we have found will help in that endeavor."

"Right. Secure the bags of evidence in the van." Fiona nodded to the two techs and then headed toward the vehicle. "Thank you for helping us, Grace. Tell Dr. Wilson we appreciate her cooperation."

Although she had no reason to think she'd be attacked again, Grace hurried after Fiona. Standing beside the van, she texted Logan, then removed her coveralls, and slipped on her coat. During their two weeks of Skyping, she had grown closer to Logan, and now with the dig concluded, they'd be able to spend uninterrupted time together until he returned to Texas and she to her job. One whole day and then he could drive her to Oxford.

She drew in a deep breath and turned her back on the techs chatting by Fiona's car. Why did the thought of this closeness unnerve her? Rubbing her temples helped untangle the concerns buzzing around her mind. She hadn't been this close to anyone since her husband's death. All her life she'd been labeled shy, an introvert, which didn't bother her because the characterizations were accurate.

Shoving her hand into her pockets, she nodded her head once. Yes. She'd reached a conclusion. She wanted nothing more than to be Logan's wife. If he didn't propose before he left, she would pop the question. She had to know his intentions. If not marriage, then she'd never see him again.

CHAPTER 29

The text from Grace brought a smile to Logan's lips. He'd been ready to pick her up at the dig site for hours. However, the big surprise he'd hoped to present her, hadn't panned out. He'd discovered that on such short notice, US citizens couldn't get married in England. A simple online check would have saved him a lot of time.

The next plan might be more feasible. He'd propose before he left and set a wedding date, provided Grace accepted. As he approached the site, he frowned. He was almost certain she would, but there was always the possibility…

Nope. Don't go there, man.

Grace and the other techs loaded equipment into the van. He parked so his headlights shone on the group. She turned and gave him a wave. The sight of her in her pink coat and her black hair loose sent his heart rate into overdrive. He climbed out of the car and opened his arms. She hugged him and then looked up at him, her lips inviting. He kissed her and reluctantly released her when he heard a wolf whistle coming from the van.

Once she was settled beside him in the passenger seat, he asked, "Can you tell me what you found today?"

"Three males, buried after May 2017."

"You can be that accurate?"

She chuckled then sobered. "I'm good but not that good. I found a ticket stub to a concert dated May 2017. The men were murdered."

"Presumably by Martin?"

"We can make that assumption since his brother told us Martin buried bodies here."

"And the children? Any news?"

She reached over and set her hand on his knee. He wrapped his fingers around hers.

"They have been tentatively identified as twins who were kidnapped." Her voice broke.

"You don't have to say anymore." He squeezed her hand. "I'm sure you're tired, so let's just have a quiet meal together and tomorrow we can make time to talk. And plan. Is that okay with you?"

"Certainly. I want to shower and change first."

She said no more on the short drive to her hotel. Logan wondered if her reticence was due to fatigue or something else. The *something else* bothered him. Were her feelings toward him cooling, or was the actuality of her contract in Oxford ending and the beginning of a new job in a new city causing her to reevaluate her situation?

Tomorrow's chat now took on a whole new perspective.

~~~
~~~

As planned the previous night, Logan waited in the lobby of Grace's hotel. They were going to a café for breakfast. He stuck his hand in his pocket and clasped the small box containing his great-grandmother's ring.

Dressed in black pants and a pink sweater, she looked as elegant as if she wore a designer's outfit. The smile she gave him set his mind at rest. She hadn't changed her mind about him.

The quaint café only had a few tables but their takeaway business seemed to be booming. The waitress seated them at a small table in the back, a good place to have an intimate conversation, and took their order.

Before even sipping her coffee, Grace leaned forward and asked, "Will you come with me to church this morning?"

Logan should have been prepared for the question knowing she attended services whenever she could. "Um, I'm not sure." *Rash reply.*

"Why not?"

"Okay, I'll go to please you. I'll do anything for you."

"Wrong answer."

The waitress delivered their bacon and egg sandwiches.

Logan pushed aside his plate, his appetite suddenly gone. "What?"

"You must go to honor God. To worship Him. To show your thankfulness for His Grace and salvation through His son."

Words failed him. Of course, her answer made sense. He picked up his mug and took a gulp.

"You never told me why you're at odds with God." She nibbled on a piece of bacon but never dropped her gaze from his face.

He repeated the story of Tyler, the youth minister from his youth.

"What happened to him?"

"He was fired, moved away. His wife forgave him, and they still live in the same area."

"And the girl?"

"She left the church. Was devastated because Tyler didn't divorce his wife and marry her. I don't know anything about her life now."

Despite her diminutive size, Grace had a good appetite. She was halfway through her meal and pointed to his plate. "Your food is getting cold. I have an idea. Indulge me, please. Why did your parents divorce?"

"My dad cheated on my mom, more than once. They divorced when I was eleven." Logan forked a chunk of egg into his mouth.

"Maybe in the back of your mind, you equated your dad's actions with the youth minister's and you used their behavior to divorce you from God. You have let those two men stand between you and God. In other words, the men who caused you to leave God are closer to Him than you are."

Whoa. Too much to think about on an empty stomach. Logan finished his meal under the watchful eyes of Grace.

"The service will begin soon." She grabbed her coat. "Will you take me, Please?"

"Certainly." Logan paid the bill, slipped on his jacket, and walked with her to his car. He drove to the church building in silence.

"One more thing, Logan. Remember the story of the Prodigal Son? His father waited at the gates, daily.

He didn't go searching for him because he knew the decision to return home had to be his son's. So it is with our Heavenly Father. The decision to return to Him has to be ours. He won't force us." Grace opened her door but before climbing out, added, "I love you and that's why I gave you this mini sermon." Tears puddled in her dark eyes.

CHAPTER 30

Humbled by Grace's words, Logan parked along High Street and strolled beside the river. In his heart, he recognized she was right. If he returned to the Father like the prodigal, it had to be his decision and it had to be for the right reasons. His dad never had any interest in religion, but service to God had been Tyler's life. It wasn't inconceivable Tyler repented, and God would have accepted him back in the fold. Which added fuel to Grace's analogy. His dad and Tyler were closer to God than he was. The reminder jolted Logan's soul.

Another part of Grace's conversation stuck with him. "You allowed the actions of those men to divorce you from God." Right. He had chosen his course. He'd used his disappointment as a reason to leave the church.

A squadron of ducks swam in single file down the river. Logan grinned briefly then returned his mind to his dilemma. He hadn't fallen off the rails completely. But he was the prodigal son.

His wandering took him past the war memorial. They were prominent in most of the villages he and

Mother had visited. No one in his family except his Great-grandfather Gee had served in the military. His grandfather was drafted for Vietnam, but his heart problems excluded him.

Red poppy wreaths surrounded the base of the memorial honoring veterans from the village who'd died during WWI and WWII. Their names were inscribed on the plinth, but he couldn't read them as the memorial was behind a low chain fence, denying closer access. They had given their lives for freedom, as veterans have in conflicts since then.

Logan sat on a nearby bench. What had he given his life to? Medicine? Making money? He certainly didn't inconvenience himself for anyone. Not even his own son. No wonder Corey had to *think about* Logan's invite for Thanksgiving.

Until the false accusation, he'd had a good career, money for whatever he wanted, freedom to do pretty much anything. Although he'd achieved it all without praying once, there was an emptiness in his inner being, where his soul resided just waiting to be allowed into his life.

Mother's illness did make him reevaluate his life to a degree, but meeting Grace had been his ultimate wake-up call. Their conversation over breakfast led him to believe she loved him, but more than anything, she wanted him to return to God.

As she'd said, he had to act on his own accord and for his soul. He'd said a few short prayers over the past month, but he hadn't opened his heart to God. He'd forgotten how. One lesson he remembered Tyler had repeated over and over was that God heard all our prayers said in earnest, whether they were long soliloquies or phrases from the heart.

Bowing his head, he closed his eyes. "Father God, I come to You and ask for forgiveness for neglecting You and for straying from Your Word. Thank You for keeping me safe despite my actions. Please give me strength to continue to follow You. Bless Mother and may she have many more years with us. Thank You for Grace and bless our future together. In Jesus's name. Amen."

He raised his head and sighed. Grace and Mother would be happy with his decision. Their concerns for his soul might have spurred him along the journey, but this decision made *him* whole, and that was most important.

Minutes later, he drove to the church building and met Grace as she exited the side door.

"You look…different." She linked her arm through his.

"Good. I am different. I'm forgiven and I am no longer a prodigal."

She looked at him, her brow furrowed.

In case she hadn't heard him, he repeated, "I am no longer a prodigal."

"That's what I thought you said. Am I to assume you are no longer at odds with God? You have mended the breach?"

Overcome by emotion, he nodded, afraid his voice would crack if he spoke.

She leaned closer. "Let's get in the car."

Seated beside him, she grabbed his lapels and pulled him to her. "I am so proud of you. In the book of Luke, I think it's chapter fifteen, there's a verse that says the angels rejoice when a sinner repents." Her smile advertised her joy, but her soft lips against his told him of her love.

She pulled away. "Are you ready for lunch?"

"Not yet. Fasten your seatbelt. I have another surprise for you."

"What could be more exciting than your return God?"

He didn't reply as he drove down High Street and parked along the curb close to the bridge where he first saw her. Taking her hand, he led her onto the arched stone bridge and stopped in the middle.

"Why are we here?" Grace's quizzical expression added to her beauty.

Kneeling, he removed the box from his pocket and looked up at her. "Because I met you here, where the Windrush flows. I love you more than I thought possible, Grace. Will you accept this ring and my heart, and do me the honor of being my wife?" He opened the box and exposed the ring.

Eyes wide, she gasped. "You sneak. Yes, yes, Logan, my knight. I will marry you."

He stood and picked her up and swung her around, careful not to get too close to the edge. "You have made me the happiest man in the world."

"And, Sir Knight, you have rescued me again."

He set her down but kept his arms around her. "Again?"

"Yes, I was lost and lonely, and thought I'd never have a family."

"Hold onto your hat, girl. I want to have a family with you. As many kids as you desire." They kissed and only pulled apart when an elderly couple walking their dog crossed the bridge.

Logan slid the ring onto her finger. It would only require a small adjustment.

"It's beautiful. My birthstone."

"It was my great-grandmother's. She also had a July birthdate."

Arm in arm, they strolled back to the car.

"I want you to know I loved my late husband, but I love you with all my heart."

"And I must tell you I've been engaged before. Twice."

She stopped and turned to him. "Did I hear you correctly? Twice?"

Nodding, he held up two fingers.

"Do tell. I might change my mind" Her smile negated her words.

"Once when I was very young, just beginning med school. She was also a student, but we both realized at the same time we didn't love each other enough to get married."

"That was propitious."

"You certainly chose the right word. However, the second engagement didn't end well. I was older and should have known better. During my time with Doctors Without Borders, I proposed to another doctor. At the end of my contract with the organization, I assumed she wanted to return to America. She didn't. I left and broke up with her via a letter." He grimaced. "Not my finest moment and I've regretted it ever since."

Grace frowned. "Indeed." She tugged on his arm and began walking again. "Do you know anything about her now?"

"Yes. Thank the Lord, she's happily married and

still serving in Uganda." He stopped at his car. "Have you changed your mind about marrying me?" Gut muscles tensed in case of a negative reply, he gazed into her dark eyes.

"Open the door, please. I'm cold."

He obliged, then seated behind the wheel, he turned on the heater.

"I believe you are not the same person you were back then. You wouldn't be so callus now, would you?"

Shaking his head, he said, "I did write to her and apologized."

"Good. I want to marry you. As soon as we can make arrangements."

"Whew. You had me worried there for a minute." Relief made him chuckle. "In fact, I wanted to marry you before I went home. But it's not possible."

"Why?"

"English law. US citizens can't get married here on such short notice."

"No problem. The term ends the first week of December. I will have paperwork to complete, but I should be able to fly home the second weekend. I don't want the traditional white dress, bridesmaids et cetera. Had that once." She looked at him. "Unless you want all the trappings."

"No. I don't mind the *where*, but I would like the *when* to be soon so Mother can attend while she still knows us."

Leaning toward him, Grace cupped his face. "And I would love for Irene to help in the planning." She kissed him, a long lingering kiss that told him his revelations hadn't changed her heart one bit.

Reluctantly, he pulled away. "We can have a small

wedding or even go to the Justice of the Peace. All I care about is you saying 'I do'."

CHAPTER 31

Sanding on the platform of Oxford station and waving goodbye to Logan almost brought Grace to tears. If she'd had more than two weeks to wait until they'd be together again, she might have blubbered. Once he reached Heathrow, he would text her, and again when he boarded the plane to Austin.

By the time she reached her office, her mind was focused back on her students and their final sessions with her. Kristy was the first to notice her engagement ring.

"Oh, Dr. Gentry, it's beautiful. When's the big day?"

"Soon after I return home. Logan's mother has Alzheimer's, and we want to marry while she still knows who her son is."

"I saw you with him yesterday." Marcus settled in his favorite armchair. "What does he think about Oxford?"

"I showed him around several of our buildings. He was fascinated by the history of the university.

Especially the age of the place and the number of separate colleges." Grace opened her notebook. "Enough about Logan. Who wants to be first to discuss your essay?"

Grace listened to the arguments and comments, but her mind frequently wandered to Logan and the days she'd spent with him. She was ecstatic about his proposal, but his commitment to God pleased her more. His ring reminded her of both and her gaze strayed to her left hand more than once.

Her students had fun at her expense and teased her about her lack of concentration. Even Susan participated. "I think we should get out early today, Dr. Gentry."

"Why?"

"Your mind is not on the topic."

"Not so fast, Miss Thanh." Grace smiled and asked another question about identifying healed fractures on ancient bones. Thirty minutes later, they left, and she checked her messages. Logan was onboard his flight, seated beside two nuns. That should make for an interesting trip.

Since she wouldn't be able to Skype with him that evening, she began packing and ordered a takeaway meal of fish and chips. By midnight, she'd completed the chore, graded the latest set of essays, and jotted down questions for each student.

In the morning, she said a prayer of thanks when she read Logan's text. He'd had a safe journey during which he'd learned a lot about the life of a nun in the twenty-first century, and Corey agreed to spend Thanksgiving with him and Irene in Round Rock.

In between meeting with her students individually

to review their final essays and documenting the required assessments the department needed before she concluded her year at the university, Grace worked in the lab on the skeletal remains they had located at Salmonsbury Camp Hillfort. The sophisticated equipment provided dates for the bones, and as she predicted, they were all late Anglo-Saxon, possibly the ninth century. Except for the few remains they'd found in Tertius not associated with the teenager and two children. The lab supported her estimate of those bones being three hundred years old.

Logan had Skyped with Grace on Thanksgiving Day. Irene even participated but he said Corey was not ready yet. Which she understood. Logan seemed a bit distracted, and when she inquired, he shrugged and hinted he was having a difficult time connecting with his son.

The next week, the last week of the term, Grace and the students were having a heated discussion about features on bones associated with human activity, and how these features could be used to determine the job the person had when Dr. Wilson knocked on the office door, opened it, and peeked in.

"Dr. Gentry, I need to see you, please."

"Certainly." Grace raised her eyebrows. "We will continue this tomorrow, which will be our last meeting."

The students gathered their belongings and filed out of the room. Kristy stopped at the door. "It's been a pleasure working with you, Dr. Gentry. I want to follow in your footsteps. May I use you as a reference in the future?"

"Of course. Dr. Wilson will have my address in

Texas. And the pleasure has been mine, young lady."

Grace proceeded to Peggy's office, took a deep breath, and knocked.

"Come."

She opened the door and halted. There were two other people in the room, each holding briefcases, all official-looking.

"Dr. Gentry, I'll let my visitors introduce themselves."

The plump man wearing thick, black-rimmed glasses, nodded and said, "Mr. Smythe."

"I'm Miss O'Keefe, the lead investigator." The middle-aged woman sat and retrieved a notebook from her briefcase before setting it on the floor.

"Have a seat, Dr. Gentry." Peggy sat behind her desk.

Grace sat on the edge of the highbacked wooden chair, hands clasped in her lap. Lead investigator for what? The tight expressions on the three faces in front of her sent quivers to her stomach muscles.

O'Keefe opened her notebook. "We're here to clarify your involvement in the discovery of the modern skeletal remains found at Salmonsbury Camp Hillfort in Bourton-on-the-Water."

Grace leaned back. The details were fresh in her memory as she still regretted going home that day and leaving her students. "What do you want to know?"

"Please give us a rundown of the day," Smythe said.

"I have a journal in my office, a dig site log. It details the actions and findings of the crew blow-by-blow. I signed off on it each day."

Peggy nodded to her. "Please fetch it."

Minutes later, Grace returned, sat, and opened the journal to the date requested. "Marcus Reid, my assistant at the site, was in charge of recording every find. He also took numerous photographs of all bones and artifacts in situ and after removal. Here is the first entry of that day." Grace passed the journal to O'Keefe seated to her right. "I forwarded the photos to the detective on the scene, James McDonald. Do you need them, too?"

"We have them." Smythe stared at her over the rims of his glasses.

Huh. Their investigation began before they quizzed her.

The two investigators read the entries while O'Keefe held the book. Five long drawn-out minutes later, she asked, "All the skeletal remains you'd found up to this point were pre-modern?"

Still not accustomed to the reference UK authorities used for people determined to have died before the death of Queen Victoria, Grace almost smiled. She cleared her throat. "Yes. Anglo-Saxon, as were most others found by previous excavations."

"We are familiar with the area, Dr. Gentry."

Yes, sir. Grace crossed her legs and didn't allow Smythe's words or stare to intimidate her.

"Do your students know the difference between ancient bones and pre-modern bones?"

Grace bit her bottom lip. Here was the crux of the problem. "Yes. In a lab setting under powerful lighting, with all dirt and debris removed."

"What can you say in defense of them removing the bones from the site?"

"We did that with all the remains. We'd

experienced some vandalism and needed to protect our finds. The bones located that day had no soft tissue attached, no tendons or ligaments. In the muted light under the canopy, on an overcast day, and in an area where we'd only found ancient bones, I believe they acted responsibly. They always used appropriate excavation techniques, and I believe the integrity of the site was preserved by the photographs taken and by the detailed log entries."

O'Keefe turned to Dr. Wilson. "Do you believe Dr. Gentry acted per excavation protocol?"

Grace dared not look at her boss. Here, as the saying went, the rubber would meet the road.

"Yes. Before she left the site that day due to illness, she reported to me. I agreed she could leave Mr. Reid in charge." She raised her chin. "Dr. Gentry has my full support."

O'Keefe and Smythe stuffed their notebooks into their briefcases and stood. She said, "You'll have our report before the end of term."

~~~

The waiting tainted Grace's last few days in Oxford. However, she received news from Fiona that lightened her mood.

"I have updates on our burial sites in Bourton. First of all, DI McDonald told me Martin Evans confessed to murdering his partner and burying him on the mound at Solmonsbury. They'd been robbing area homes fifteen years ago, and Billy, um, I forget his surname, got greedy. Martin also disposed of the leather jewelry pouch along with some items he didn't think were valuable, and I think he said a backpack.

"The twins were abducted but died when he
~~~

administered too much sedative. McDonald said Martin was devastated, however, that didn't stop him from keeping the ransom money. The three men we found beneath the children had been Martin's gaming chums who tried to cheat him. He admitted booze was involved and he'd killed them in a fit of rage."

"I guess my team and I got off easy with only threats of violence. Did McDonald mention Ivan and the part he played?"

"Martin was quick to add his brother only helped him bury the body by the lake and wasn't involved in the other deaths. Both men are in custody."

"Did Martin mention why he chose those two sites?"

"He did. According to McDonald, he was eager to provide information and answer questions. After he killed his partner, he was going to dump his body in one of the lakes but noticed the ground on the mound which looked freshly plowed."

"I suppose that makes sense. What about the twins and the three men?"

"He chose the site along Rissington Road because it was secluded and he figured the coppice wouldn't be disturbed, which proved to be true."

"The what?" Grace hadn't heard that word before.

"Coppice, or copse. Yeah, it's an old word for a grove of trees that won't be completely cut down."

After Grace ended the call, she opened the logbook and turned to the pages the investigators had focused on. At least her absence and her students' actions hadn't compromised the scene, and the right man was in jail.

Sitting on her small balcony overlooking the spired-filled city, Grace sipped her tea. Her time in

England was a highlight in her life thus far and she prayed she'd have many more with Logan. Considering what awaited her in Texas, she had no inclination to visit any of the touristy places in London, not even Harrod's. She had few qualms about her future. Until she and Logan married, she'd live with Irene.

The only niggling doubt involved the report from O'Keefe and Smythe. Their conclusion could affect her future career.

CHAPTER 32

It took Logan two days before he ventured into the bedroom Corey had used while he visited the previous week. Their time together hadn't panned out as he'd hoped. Corey did seem to enjoy his time with his grandmother, but any reply to a question Logan posed was met with a grunt.

Logan had no one to blame but himself. Although he'd made sure Sylvie, Corey's mother, always had sufficient funds to care for their son, he'd seldom visited. While stripping the bed, he noticed a piece of paper tucked under the pillow. He opened it cautiously, not sure what Corey might have done.

To his surprise, Corey had written him a letter.

Dear Dad:

I really didn't want to come, but Mother persuaded me to, and now I'm glad. Grandmother is a hoot. I promised to write to her since she doesn't use email. I won't mind if you read the letters. Mother told me you supported her financially and she never blamed you for anything. She even said you agreed to marry her, but I'm grateful you didn't. Frank is a super Dad—sorry if that hurts your feelings.

I do want to get to know you better. And I want to meet Grace. Invite me to the wedding.

Love, Corey.

Logan plopped onto the bed. He hadn't expected anything positive from Corey. Mother was probably responsible for the kid's change of heart. No matter, Logan said a prayer of thanks and folded the letter. He had the perfect place for it—in his new Bible.

Part of his problem during Corey's visit had been his distracted behavior. The day before Thanksgiving, Wayne had phoned to say the mother of one of his former patients was accusing him of sexually molesting her daughter. His words acted as a sucker punch to the gut.

Nothing could be further from the truth. Besides the fact Logan would never do anything so despicable, he'd made it a requirement a nurse accompany every patient he examined. Although the accusation would not hold up under scrutiny, it was another brick thrown at his reputation. He might never be able to practice again.

Any case of sexual misconduct had to be taken seriously and investigated. Logan knew that but the false allegation weighed him down.

After making up the bed, Logan emailed Wayne and asked for updates.

In response, Wayne called. "I suggest you preempt the cops showing up at your door. Meet me at the station in Round Rock, in say, thirty minutes. Do you have a calendar from your last year in Houston?"

"I have the office laptop. And the appointments are still on my phone."

"Bring both."

Logan sat beside Mother on the sofa. She was doing so well and loved having Verna in the house. "I have to go into town and might be gone a while."

"No problem, son. Verna is taking me to deliver the crocheted blanket I made for Marge's grandbaby."

"Have fun." He kissed her on the cheek and hurried to his vehicle. Gone a while? Hopefully a few hours and not days.

Wayne waited outside the station.

Logan parked, grabbed the laptop, and met his lawyer on the sidewalk. "When was the incident supposed to have happened?" He'd already charged the computer when Wayne made the initial call days ago and opened it to the schedule page.

Wayne checked his notes. "The morning of July 26."

"Not possible." He closed the laptop and headed toward the doors.

"Wait. Give me a heads up, please."

"I did not see any patients that day. In fact, I didn't enter the office. Check with the office manager. It's Mother's birthday and because of her disease, I spent the day with her. Don't know how many more birthdays she'll have. We went to Six Flags Fiesta Texas in San Antonio." Logan chuckled. "Would you believe she wanted to ride the roller coaster?"

"Okay. Remember to let me do the talking. Let's not give away any details. The woman might change her mind about the date." Wayne punched Logan's arm. "Ready?"

He nodded and stepped inside.

Wayne provided the necessary information, and soon a police officer showed them to an interview room. "A detective will be with you shortly."

Checking the time frequently did not help the minutes move any faster. Finally, a woman entered the room, set a folder on the table, and sat opposite Logan. "I'm Detective Rosalie Jackson. I believe you want to make a statement, Mr. Quinn, uh, sorry, Dr. Quinn."

Wayne asked, "Is this meeting being recorded?"

"No, but it can be if you so desire."

"Yes, and if you don't mind, I'll record it on my phone, too."

She nodded. "Go ahead, Dr. Quinn."

"Not so fast." Wayne produced a file from his briefcase. "Here is a copy of the charge leveled against my client. It states that a patient of his was molested on the morning of July 26 of this year in his consulting room in Houston."

"Wait a minute. Why are you here and not in Houston?"

"My client has since moved to Round Rock, and we want this bogus charge dropped before it goes any further."

The detective leaned back and frowned. "It won't be that simple, Mr. Hammond. I need to contact the authorities in Houston."

Logan held up his hand and looked at Wayne. He moved closer, and whispered, "Not Houston. Cypress which is served by the Harris County Sheriff's Department."

"Thanks for reminding me." Wayne repeated the information Logan shared.

"I'll contact them, then. Be back as soon as I can." Detective Jackson left the room.

Wayne turned off his phone recorder. "We might be here a while."

Logan opened his mouth to speak but Wayne shook his head. "They might still be recording. Don't say a word."

The back and forth between the Harris County Sheriff's office and the detective resulted in questions for Logan which Wayne answered, or the clarification of details.

Two hours into the process, she entered the room again and sat. "I see you have your laptop. Are your appointments listed on it?"

Logan nodded.

"When did your lawyer apprise you of the date in question?"

Wayne nudged him. "I'll answer that. Today, outside this building. And I will swear that my client made no changes on his computer."

"How about the name of the accuser?"

"We don't have that information."

"I can provide that to you now." She flipped a page in the folder. "Paula Kennedy."

"And her daughter?"

"Um, Pauline Kennedy."

"What about the reason she brought her daughter in to see the doctor?"

Jackson scanned another sheet of paper. "Apparently, Pauline broke her arm, the left ulna and radius, which didn't set correctly. Mrs. Kennedy wanted Dr. Quinn to fix the problem with surgery."

Logan shrugged. "I don't remember the names of all my patients, let alone their parents. But..." He hit the table with his fist. "I would have remembered *that* patient. My first action would have been to track down who did the original setting of her arm before agreeing to any surgery. And I don't recall ever doing that. Therefore, I'm certain this Pauline was never in my consulting room."

"We can produce the office patient records." Wayne turned to Logan. "What happened to 'don't say anything'?"

He had to defend himself. Rolling his eyes, he whispered, "The records are with my personal belongings in a storage facility in Cypress."

"My client's records will show that he did not have a patient by that name and since he's only received that name now, there is no way he could have destroyed any documents connected to her."

The detective left the room, and Wayne hunched over the table. "I'm hungry. How about you?"

Logan nodded.

"When she returns, I'll ask for refreshments."

However, a few minutes later, she opened the door. "You're free to go, Dr. Quinn. We'll be in touch when the Harris County Sheriff has gathered more information. Just don't leave the state."

As soon as Logan arrived home late that afternoon,

he chanced a Skype session with Grace. Although two hours past their usual time, he hoped she'd still be awake.

"Hey, Dr. Quinn." She exaggerated a look at her watch. "What's the meaning of this?"

"You won't believe what happened today." He gave her a condensed version of events. "As if I needed any more hits to my reputation."

"I'm sorry that's happened to you. I also have a dilemma. Yesterday, two investigators questioned me about the day I left my students at the dig, and they found skeletal remains that were not ancient. The dig site *police* are supposed to have their report ready before the end of term."

Despite the dire news, Logan laughed. "We can cry on each other's shoulders, my love."

"If not so serious, the situation would be funny. Both our careers are on the line."

"I have an idea. If we can't work in our desired fields, why don't we open a travel agency? We can use our expertise and take groups of people to the UK and tour the Roman ruins. You can explain everything, and I can, um, take their photographs. Or professional pictures of the sites."

She chuckled and shook her head. "Oh, Logan my dear, that would be interesting. But back to reality, if I'm cleared, I'll be on a flight next week."

He stared into her eyes. "Father God, please help us clear our names so we can serve you as an anthropologist and a doctor."

"Amen." Tears glistened in Grace's eyes. "That's the first time I've heard you pray."

"And it won't be the last."

~~~

To help take his mind off his woes, Logan checked out apartments for rent online. Although he had good credit, he didn't have a job, and several agencies were hesitant to rent to him. One agency finally accepted his bank records which showed his hefty balance, and his credible references.

The two-bedroom apartment was in the southern part of the city, close to the Interstate, which would make Grace's commute easier. After signing the lease, he arranged for his furniture to be brought from Cypress.

By the end of the week, Logan had used up all his creativity in sorting through the many photos he'd taken on their trip. Mother wanted a few enlarged and while they were at the store paying for the frames, Wayne called.

Logan struggled to breathe and clutched the shirt over his heart to slow its pounding. "Any news, Wayne?"

"Are you sitting down?"

Not the words he wanted to hear. "No." He ushed Mother out of the store and through the parking lot.

"Never mind. You've been cleared of all charges."

Logan leaned against his car. "Cleared, as in… Whew. Praise God."

"Amen, brother. Want to know what the cops discovered?"

"Definitely." He opened the passenger door. "Wait in here, Mother. I need to finish this conversation."

"No problem, son."

"Tell me, please."

"Okay, so they questioned Mrs. Kennedy and
~~~

noted several inconsistencies in her story."

The excitement in Wayne's voice brought a grin to Logan's face.

"Here's the cherry on top. She doesn't have a daughter. She doesn't have any children. And she admitted to being paid to make the accusation."

"Paid by whom?"

"The police tracked down the person and he's related to Adrian Kerns."

"So…so I can work again. I'm… Thank you for all your help and support."

"That's what you pay me for. Go celebrate. When's Grace arriving?"

"She hasn't given me a date yet."

"You'd better invite me to the wedding."

"I will. Bye."

Before Logan shared his great news with Grace during their Skype session that afternoon, he asked about her situation.

"Still waiting on the report, but I'm going to book my flight for next week. No matter what they decide, I'm coming home."

Home to marry him. After saying goodbye, Logan closed his laptop and fell to his knees. With or without a job, he would be content with having Grace at his side.

EPILOGUE

December 23rd

Dressed in a long, champagne-pink satin gown with a full skirt, Grace descended the stairs. Logan stood at the bottom, wearing a black tux rented for the occasion.

"You look like a dream, my darling." He held out his hand.

"And you cleaned up pretty good yourself."

He kissed her cheek. "Your carriage awaits." He draped a thick white shawl around her shoulders and ushered her outside.

The cottage they'd rented in Bourton-on-the-Water was two blocks from the river, too far to walk in the frosty early evening air. The professional photographer he'd hired agreed to drive them to their destination— the bridge over the Windrush where Logan had first seen Grace.

Seated in the backseat of Terry's SUV, he clasped her hand. So much had happened since he'd last visited the village. Grace was exonerated before she left Oxford, so when they married at the Justice of the Peace's office in Round Rock three days ago, neither one had a cloud of doubt hanging over their heads. And when they returned home, he'd begin in a new practice with his friend, Dr. Dana Booth.

Only Mother and a few friends attended the quick ceremony, but it didn't matter. They were man and wife spending their honeymoon in Bourton.

"Here we are." Terry opened the back door and helped Grace out. "This is as close as I can get to the bridge."

"It's fine, thanks." Logan crooked his elbow and Grace placed her small hand on his arm. "Okay, Terry. You know the photos we want. Just tell us what to do and where to stand, et cetera." He guided Grace onto the middle of the bridge.

"I will. The lighted Christmas tree in the middle of the river will feature in most of them."

It seemed as if Terry took a hundred photos, but he often asked Grace if she was cold or needed a break.

Back in his vehicle with the heater on high, he showed them the spectacular photos. Not only did Grace look like a princess, the Christmas tree and other holiday decorations on the buildings close to the river enhanced their wedding pictures.

"Great job, Terry." Grace huddled under the shawl. "I hope there's a fire in the restaurant we're going to for dinner."

Logan had made reservations for a special meal at one of the hotels. Terry dropped them off at the door, and they were shown to a secluded table close to the fireplace.

Although he'd chosen the menu, Logan couldn't remember what he'd eaten. He was ecstatically happy and couldn't take his eyes off his bride.

They walked back to the cottage, and later, wearing matching pajamas, they sat on the sofa in front of the fireplace, sipping spiced apple cider.

"Logan, this day has been wonderful. You are a man of many surprises."

"I aim to please."

"Bourton will always hold a special place in my heart."

He drew her closer. "Me too." He paused. "Why don't we make Bourton-on-the-Water our place? Bring our children here during the summers."

"That would be lovely. We could also try other villages."

"No. This is where the Windrush flows, and without the Windrush, there'd be no bridges, and without the bridges, I wouldn't have met you."

THE END

Dear Reader:

I had such fun writing this book. It is the first romance I've written where the hero and heroine fall for each other quickly. Do you believe in love at first sight? The experience hits Logan smack between the eyes.

When I first met my husband, I knew he was the one. We were married for 48 years!

If ever you visit the Cotswolds and need a wonderful place to stay, check out the cottages I mentioned.

If you liked this novel, please consider leaving a review. Reviews are important to authors.

Sincerely,

Valerie Massey Goree

Sign up for my monthly newsletter:
https://bit.ly/VGJoinMyCommunity
Check out my Facebook author page.
www.facebook.com/ValerieMasseyGoree
Visit my website: www.valeriegoreeauthor.com
My books are also featured at:
www.goodreads.com/search? and
https://www.bookbub.com/search?

Bio:
Award winner Valerie Massey Goree resides in the beautiful Hill Country, northwest of San Antonio,

After serving as missionaries in her home country of Zimbabwe and raising two children, Valerie and her husband, Glenn, a native Texan, moved to Texas. She worked in the public school system for many years, focusing on students with special needs. Now retired, Valerie spends her time writing, traveling, and spoiling her grandchildren.

Valerie loves to hear from her readers.

Check Valerie's website to learn more about her romantic suspense novels and Glenn's non-fiction books:
www.valeriegoreeauthor.com

All my books and live links:

Deceive Me Once

Colors of Deceit:

Stolen Lives Trilogy:

1.Weep in the Night:

2.Day of Reckoning:

3.Justice at Dawn

Forever Under Blue Skies:
of Time

Every Hidden Thing